MAN ADVANTAGE

LADY HEARTSWELL

CENTURIA BOOKS LLC

CONTENTS

Chapter One

THE SOFTEST FRACTURE

POV: Mina

The data points were irrefutable: Mercer and Rook were exclusively homosexual, aggressively devoted to one another, and physically capable of snapping her spine like a dry twig. So why was Mina's amygdala misfiring so catastrophically?

Rain lashed against the grand entrance of the arena, turning the world into a gray blur of water and asphalt. The donor gala thrummed on the other side of the glass doors—a world of champagne flutes, seven-figure checks, and people who didn't ruin their evening wear by kneeling in a gutter.

Mina was not one of those people.

A pitiful, high-pitched *mewl* cut through the storm again. It wasn't a hallucination. There was life in the storm drain, tiny and desperate.

She didn't hesitate. The logic of self-preservation that usually governed her life short-circuited. She dropped to her knees. The wet pavement soaked instantly through the thin, cheap fabric of her tights. Mud coated her shins. The icy water bit at her skin, but she jammed her arm into the darkness of the drain, her fingers searching blindly in the muck.

"Come on," she whispered, her voice cracking. "I've got you."

Her fingertips brushed wet fur. The kitten hissed, a vibration of pure terror, but Mina lunged. Her hand closed around the scruff of a neck no bigger than her thumb. She hauled the creature out, curling her body around it to shield it from the deluge. It was a soaked scrap of black fur, shivering so violently it shook in her hands.

She sat back on her heels, gasping, mud streaked across her cheek and slime dripping from her elbow. She probably looked deranged. A biology major playing savior in the slush.

Then the air pressure dropped.

It wasn't a meteorological shift. It was a displacement of mass. A shadow fell over her, blocking out the harsh security lights, spanning so wide it felt like an eclipse.

Mina looked up. And up.

Mercer stood there.

The captain of the team. The golden god of the ice. He wasn't wearing his jersey tonight. He wore a charcoal suit that cost more than her entire tuition, the fabric straining across shoulders that seemed engineered to carry the weight of the world—or crush it.

He was terrifying. He was beautiful.

Biology was a cruel mistress. It didn't care about orientation or availability. It only cared about the specimen standing above her. Mina's gaze traveled up the long, powerful columns of his legs, encased in wool that clung to thighs thick with muscle. His torso was a V-shape of violence wrapped in silk, tapering to a waist she wanted to wrap her legs around, broadening out to a chest that could act as a battering ram.

He wasn't just a man; he was an apex predator in formal wear. His hands hung at his sides—massive, scarred things. Hands that choked hockey sticks and, if the rumors were true, his partner's throat. The veins on the back of his hands stood out like ropes, tracking up into his cuffs. Those fingers were long, blunt, and capable of terrible things. Mina's mouth watered. A sick, heavy pulse throbbed between her legs, a traitorous ache that ignored the freezing rain.

Look at him, her brain whispered, abandoning all dignity. *He could break you in half and you'd thank him for the efficiency.*

Mercer stared down at her. His face was a mask of cold disdain, the nose crooked from one too many pucks to the face, his jaw clenched tight enough to grind diamonds. He looked at her like she was a stain on the concrete.

"What are you doing?" His voice was a low rumble, barely audible over the rain, but it vibrated in the hollow of her chest.

Mina scrambled to stand, clutching the kitten against the ruined front of her dress. "I... it was drowning."

Mercer's gaze dropped to the shivering ball of fur.

The disgust on his face vanished, replaced by something unreadable. He stepped closer. The scent of him hit her—rain, expensive sandalwood, and the sharp, metallic tang of pure alpha dominance. It made her knees weak. It made her want to fall back down into the mud just to show him her belly.

He reached out.

Mina flinched, expecting a blow or a shove. Instead, those massive, dangerous hands cupped the kitten. He took the animal from her with a gentleness that stopped her heart. His thumb, thick and calloused, stroked the tiny head. The kitten, which had been hissing at Mina, instantly went silent, melting into the heat of his palm.

"Stupid thing," Mercer murmured to the cat. His voice dropped an octave, turning into a rough purr that scraped pleasantly against Mina's nerve endings. He tucked the kitten inside his jacket, against the warmth of his chest, shielding it completely. "You don't belong out here in the cold."

For a second, Mina watched him, entranced. The monster had a soft underbelly. He was kind. He was saving the weak. A spark of hope ignited in her chest—maybe he wasn't as cruel as the tabloids said. Maybe he would look at her with that same protective warmth.

Then he turned his eyes back to her.

The warmth died instantly. The ice returned, harder and sharper than before.

He looked at her wet hair, plastering her skull. He looked at the mud smearing her dress. He looked at her trembling lips. He didn't see a savior. He saw trash.

"You look like a drowned rat," he said flatly.

The insult landed like a physical blow, but instead of recoiling, Mina felt a flush of heat sear through her veins. He was looking at her. The great Mercer, who never looked at women, was looking at her. Even his contempt felt like a gift. It was heavy and focused, pinning her in place.

He stepped into her personal space. He was so large he blotted out the world. Mina had to crane her neck back, her spine arching involuntarily. She was five feet of awkwardness; he was six-six of sculpted aggression. The size difference was laughable. It was erotic.

"Please," she stammered, her voice barely a whisper. "I just need to go back in and dry off. My coat is in the cloakroom."

Mercer didn't move out of her way. He loomed closer. He raised a hand.

Mina froze.

His thumb, the same one that had just gentled the kitten, pressed against her cheekbone. The skin there was rough, the pad of his finger hot and hard. He swiped downward, slow and deliberate, dragging a smear of mud away from her eye.

It was an intimate gesture. A lover's touch.

It was sickeningly sweet.

Mina's breath hitched, trapping itself in her throat. She leaned into the touch without permission, her eyes fluttering shut. *He's touching me. He's cleaning me.* It felt like a benediction.

"You're pathetic," Mercer whispered, his voice silky with malice. His thumb pressed harder, digging into her soft flesh, holding her face still so he could inspect her flaws. "Look at you. Shaking like a leaf because a man is standing near you."

Mina's eyes snapped open. His blue gaze bored into hers, dissecting her biology. He could smell it. He had to. He could smell the fear, and beneath it, the thick, cloying scent of her arousal.

He didn't pull his hand away. He rubbed the dirt between his thumb and forefinger, inspecting the filth he'd taken off her skin.

"Rook hates clutter," Mercer said, his tone conversational, as if explaining why he had to drown a sack of puppies. "And he hates messes. If you walk back into that gala looking like this, you'll offend him. And I don't like it when Rook is offended."

"I... I can clean up," Mina whispered. She wanted to lick his thumb. The thought was insane, a parasite in her brain, but she wanted to taste the salt of his skin and the mud he'd wiped from hers. She wanted to prove she could be clean for them.

Mercer smiled. It wasn't a nice smile. It was a baring of straight, white teeth that promised violence.

"No," he said. "You can't. You're messy by nature, little girl. I can see it in your eyes. You're soft. Fragile. You bleed too easily."

He finally dropped his hand, and the loss of contact made Mina's skin scream. The cold air rushed back in, leaving her shivering worse than before.

"Go home," Mercer commanded, turning his back on her. He adjusted his jacket where the kitten was nestled safe and warm. "The adults are talking inside. The nursery is closed."

He walked toward the heavy glass doors, the security guards stepping aside instantly to let the king pass.

Mina stood in the rain, water dripping off her nose, mud drying on her cheek where he had touched her. She should be furious. She should be humiliated. She had just saved a life, and he had treated her like something he scraped off his boot.

But as the door swung shut, cutting off the golden light of the gala, Mina didn't feel angry.

She lifted a trembling hand to her cheek, pressing her palm against the spot his thumb had burned. A dark, twisted gratitude blossomed in her chest, heavy and sweet like rotting fruit.

He touched me, she thought, the realization making her thighs clamp together against the empty ache. *He thinks I'm filth, but he touched me.*

She stared at the closed door, the image of his broad back burned into her retinas. He was a monster. He was cruel. He belonged to another man.

And God help her, she wanted him to do it again.

*

Mina didn't go home.

The rejection had been absolute, an eviction from the garden of the elite, but biology was a persistent glitch. She found a service entrance, a heavy steel door propped open with a cinderblock where the catering staff smoked. She slipped inside, a ghost in the machine of the arena.

She navigated the concrete labyrinth of the back hallways, the roar of the HVAC system masking the squelch of her wet shoes. She knew the layout. She'd studied the blueprints of the stadium for an astrophysics project on acoustics last semester. There was a staff restroom near the VIP suites. If she could just wash the mud off, dry her hair under the hand dryer... maybe she could salvage the night. Maybe she could sneak back in just to watch him from the shadows.

Just to see if he looked at her again.

Delusional. She was delusional.

The corridor ahead was dim, the recessed lighting turned low for the gala ambiance. Voices drifted toward her. Low. Angry.

Mina stopped. She pressed herself into a shallow alcove, trying to make her small body disappear.

"I told you to leave it alone, Rook."

The voice was Mercer's. It wasn't the silky, cruel purr he'd used on her. It was sharp, jagged with frustration.

"Don't tell me what to do, Cap." The second voice was deeper, rougher. A growl that sounded like gravel in a blender. Rook. The Enforcer.

Mina peeked around the corner.

They were there. Just ten feet away.

Mercer had the kitten—no, the kitten was gone. He must have handed it off to a staffer. Now, his hands were free, and they were shoved against Rook's chest.

Rook was a mountain. If Mercer was a statue of cold perfection, Rook was a landslide. His hair was messy, dark curls falling into eyes that burned with a chaotic, frenzied energy. His tie was undone, hanging loose around a neck thick enough to withstand a mesmerizing amount of force.

They weren't kissing. This wasn't the tender, romantic love the magazines profiled. This was war.

"You're spiraling," Mercer hissed, shoving Rook. The force of it would have knocked a normal man down; Rook just rocked back on his heels, a dark grin splitting his face.

"I'm bored, Mercer," Rook snapped back, stepping into Mercer's space. He grabbed Mercer's lapels, bunching the expensive fabric in his fists. "I'm bored of the suits. I'm bored of the talk. I need to hit something."

"Not here," Mercer warned. He didn't pull away. He leaned in, their foreheads almost touching. The aggression coming off them was palpable. It radiated in waves, a raw, unfiltered heat that made the air in the hallway taste like ozone.

"Then take me home," Rook growled. "Take me home and put me on my knees. Make me shut up."

Mina's breath caught. The explicit demand hung in the air, heavy and wet.

Mercer sneered. "I tried that this morning. You didn't submit. You fought me."

"Because you're getting soft," Rook taunted. He released one of Mercer's lapels to ghost a hand down the front of Mercer's trousers. It wasn't gentle. It was a grope, a challenge. "You can't handle me anymore."

Mercer snarled. He grabbed Rook's wrist, twisting it away with a violence that made Mina wince. He slammed Rook backward.

Rook hit the wall with a dull thud. A picture frame rattled.

"I will break your arm," Mercer threatened, pinning Rook's wrist to the wall above his head.

"Do it," Rook breathed. His head fell back, exposing his throat. He looked wrecked, desperate, high on the conflict. "Fucking do it."

Mina couldn't look away. She was witnessing a car crash of testosterone and dominance. They were tearing each other apart because neither could occupy the submissive space. Two alphas fighting for the throne, and the friction was generating enough heat to burn the building down.

She should leave. She was intruding on a private, volatile moment between two men who hated outsiders.

But her feet were lead. Her blood was rushing in her ears, a roaring tide. Watching them... seeing the way Mercer's suit jacket strained as he held Rook against the wall, seeing the wild hunger in Rook's eyes... it wired directly into her nervous system.

She let out a breath. A mistake. A tiny, soft exhalation of pure want.

Rook's head snapped toward her.

His eyes were dark, dilated so wide the irises were barely visible. He spotted her instantly in the shadows.

Mercer followed his gaze.

Mina shrank back, her heart hammering against her ribs like a trapped bird. She was caught.

Rook didn't look angry. He looked... interested. A slow, predatory curiosity dawned on his face. He pushed Mercer's hand away—Mercer let him go, his own gaze narrowing as he zeroed in on Mina.

"Well, well," Rook drawled, pushing off the wall. He smoothed his shirt, though the chaotic energy still vibrated off him. "What do we have here? A spy?"

Mina couldn't speak. Her throat had closed up.

Rook took a step toward her. Then another. He moved differently than Mercer. Mercer was controlled power; Rook was loose, a live wire snapping on the pavement.

"I... I was just..." Mina tried to retreat, but her back hit the rear of the alcove.

Rook loomed over her. He sniffed the air.

"She smells like rain," Rook said, glancing back at Mercer. "And mud."

"I told her to leave," Mercer said coldly. He stayed back, crossing his arms. He looked bored, but his eyes were tracking every micro-movement Mina made. "She doesn't listen. A bad habit."

"I like bad habits," Rook murmured. He leaned down, placing a hand on the wall beside her head. He was huge. Up close, he was overwhelming. A faint scar cut through his eyebrow, and his nose had a bump in the bridge. He smelled like sweat and expensive scotch.

Mina trembled. "I'm sorry. I'm leaving."

"Are you?" Rook's voice dropped. He lowered his face until he was nose-to-nose with her. "You watched. You like to watch, little mouse?"

Mina nodded. She couldn't lie to him. It felt impossible. "Yes."

The honesty seemed to surprise him. He blinked, then that dark grin returned. "Mercer, she likes to watch."

"She's a child, Rook. Leave it," Mercer said, though he took a step closer. The magnet was pulling him in, too.

"She's not a child," Rook whispered. His gaze dropped to her mouth, then lower, to the pulse jumping frantically in her throat. "She's terrified."

He inhaled deeply, drawing her scent into his lungs.

"God," Rook groaned, the sound vibrating in his chest. "She smells... sweet. Like sugar and fear."

Mina's knees gave out. She slumped against the wall, sliding down an inch. Rook's body crowded her, blocking out the light, blocking out escape. The heat coming off him was intoxicating. It was a furnace. She wanted to crawl inside it.

The logical part of her brain—the scientist—was screaming that this was dangerous. These men were on the edge of violence. They were frustrated, sexually aggressive, and she was the only object in the room they could both agree on.

But the other part of her? The part that had thanked Mercer for wiping the mud from her face? That part was singing.

See me, she begged silently, staring up into Rook's wild eyes. *Break me if you have to, just don't stop looking at me.*

Rook's hand moved. He didn't touch her face like Mercer had. He tangled his fingers in her damp hair, gripping the back of her skull. It wasn't gentle. It was a claim.

"Cap," Rook said, his voice strained, dragged out of a tight throat. "Come here."

Mercer hesitated. The elitist, the snob, the man who only wanted hard muscle and sharp angles. But he moved. He walked into the alcove, closing the trap.

Now she was bracketed by them. Wall behind her. Rook in front. Mercer flanking.

Mercer looked down at her. His blue eyes were ice, but the pupils were blown wide. He looked at Rook's hand in her hair. He looked at Mina's parted lips.

"She's filthy," Mercer said again. It sounded less like an insult and more like a complaint about a meal he was about to eat anyway.

"I don't care," Rook rasped. He tightened his grip on her hair, tilting her head back, exposing her throat to both of them.

Mina whimpered. The sound was small, pathetic, and it acted like a starter pistol.

Rook crashed his mouth down on hers.

It wasn't a kiss. It was a collision. It was a robbery. He tasted of scotch and rage. His lips were hard, unyielding, bruising hers against her teeth. He didn't ask for entrance; his tongue swept into her mouth, claiming the space, hunting for her taste.

Mina's hands flew up, landing on his chest. It was like pushing against a brick wall. She didn't push him away; she clutched his shirt, holding on for dear life as the world spun.

It lasted five seconds. An eternity.

Rook tore his mouth away, gasping for air. He stared at her, his eyes wide, shocked. He looked like he'd just touched a live wire.

"Fuck," he breathed. He looked at his hand, still tangled in her blonde hair. He looked at her swollen lips.

Mercer was staring at her mouth. He looked furious. He looked hungry.

"What did you do?" Mercer demanded, his voice low and lethal, directed at Mina. "What is that?"

"I... I don't know," Mina whispered. Her lips throbbed. Her body was humming, a high-pitched frequency of need that drowned out everything else.

Rook stepped back, releasing her hair as if she burned him. He looked at Mercer. "Did you smell it?"

Mercer didn't answer. He reached out, grabbing Mina's chin. His grip was hard. He tilted her face left, then right, inspecting the damage Rook had done.

"You're bleeding," Mercer noted.

Mina tasted copper. Rook had split her lip.

Mercer's thumb brushed the small drop of blood on her lower lip. He stared at it. For a terrifying second, Mina thought he was going to lick it off. She wanted him to. She wanted his mouth where Rook's had been.

Instead, Mercer wiped the blood away, then wiped his thumb on his expensive trousers.

"Get out of here," Mercer said. His voice was shaking. A tiny tremor in the tectonic plates of his control. "Run, little mouse. Before we change our minds."

He grabbed Rook by the shoulder and shoved him toward the exit, away from her.

Mina didn't have to be told twice.

She ran.

She scrambled past them, her shoes slapping against the concrete, her breath tearing at her lungs. She burst out of the service door and back into the rain, the cold water feeling like a shock against her overheated skin.

She didn't stop running until she reached the bus stop three blocks away. She collapsed onto the bench, hugging her knees to her chest.

She was cold. She was wet. She was ruined.

She brought her fingers to her lips, touching the spot where the monster had kissed her.

The data points had changed.

Hypothesis: Mercer and Rook were exclusively gay.

Observation: Rook had kissed her like he wanted to devour her soul. Mercer had touched her like she was a precious, dirty secret.

Conclusion: She was in so much trouble.

Mina closed her eyes and let the rain wash over her, a sick, sweet smile touching her lips. She was terrified.

She couldn't wait to see them again.

Chapter Two

The Soft Aberration

POV: Mercer

The silence in the Range Rover was heavy enough to choke on.

Usually, the drive home from a gala involved Rook vibrating with excess kinetic energy, tearing at his tie, complaining about the donors, or threatening to put his fist through the dashboard if I didn't drive faster. Usually, I spent the ride calculating the exact amount of force required to subdue him once we crossed the threshold of the penthouse.

Tonight, Rook stared out the window. He was perfectly, terrifyingly still.

He had one hand raised to his face. His thumb traced the curve of his bottom lip, over and over again. A grotesque, repetitive motion. He looked like an addict trying to preserve the last trace of a high.

I gripped the steering wheel until the leather creaked.

My own skin felt too tight. Itched. The sensation crawled under my suit, a localized fever centered in my chest and lower belly. It was biology. Just chemicals. I was a rational man, a strategist. I understood cause and effect.

Cause: A girl the size of a keychain ornament.

Effect: A nuclear meltdown of my entire nervous system.

It didn't make sense. I liked hard things. I liked the scrape of stubble, the bruise of muscle against muscle, the violent friction of Rook fighting me for control. I didn't like soft. I didn't like *women*. They were shrill, fragile variables that cluttered the equation.

But this one...

Mina.

The name sat in my head like a piece of candy dissolving on the tongue. Sickeningly sweet.

I glanced at Rook again. He hadn't blinked in a mile.

"Stop touching your mouth," I snapped. The words came out harsher than intended, scraping my throat.

Rook didn't drop his hand. He turned his head slowly, his dark curls falling over his forehead. His eyes were blown wide, the pupils swallowing the brown irises until they looked like black holes.

"She tasted like rain water," Rook whispered. His voice was wrecked. "And sugar. Cheap, processed sugar. The kind that rots your teeth."

My jaw locked. A sharp, hot spike of jealousy drove itself between my ribs. Not because he kissed a girl—we had no rules about women because women never mattered—but because he had tasted her, and I hadn't.

"She was filthy," I said, forcing cold detachment into my tone. "A mess."

"She was perfect." Rook's hand drifted down to his lap. He shifted in the seat. The fabric of his dress pants pulled tight across his thighs. He was hard. Painfully, visibly hard. "Did you see her hands, Merc? They were..." He held up his own massive paw, staring at it like it was an alien object. "I could crush her skull with one squeeze. She's so small. It makes me feel sick."

"You're pathetic," I muttered, but the fever in my blood spiked.

He was right. She was horrifyingly small. A little glass doll. A porcelain saint covered in mud. A stiff wind would snap her in half, and yet, she had looked at Rook like she wanted him to eat her alive.

And she had looked at me...

He touched me. I saw the thought bloom in her eyes when I wiped the dirt from her cheek. She looked at me with pure, unadulterated worship. Like I was a god descending to bless her, not a monster inspecting a stain.

It made me want to build her an altar. It made me want to lock her in a padded room where nothing sharp could ever touch her again.

I pulled the car into the private garage of our building. The tires screeched on the polished concrete. I killed the engine.

"Upstairs," I ordered. "Now."

Rook didn't argue. He didn't make a snide comment. He opened the door and unfolded his massive frame from the vehicle. We walked to the elevator in silence, but the air between us crackled. It tasted like ozone and unspent violence.

The penthouse was cold. Chrome, black leather, floor-to-ceiling glass overlooking the city. A sterile box designed for two men who lived their lives in a state of controlled aggression. There were no soft edges here. No colors.

It suddenly felt empty.

Rook walked straight to the kitchen island and gripped the edge of the marble counter. He hung his head, breathing hard.

I threw my keys on the table. The sound echoed like a gunshot. I walked up behind him.

"You're spiraling," I said, repeating the words from the arena. But this time, I didn't want to calm him down.

"I can't get the smell out of my nose," Rook rasped. He slammed his fist against the marble. "Why does she smell like that? It's biologic terrorism."

I stepped into his space. I pressed my chest against his back. Usually, this was the start of a fight. I'd grab his hair; he'd throw an elbow. We'd end up breaking furniture until one of us tapped out.

Tonight, I just wrapped an arm around his waist. I buried my nose in the junction of his neck and shoulder. I inhaled.

I smelled the expensive scotch. I smelled his sweat, sharp and masculine. But underneath it... there it was. Faint. Ghostly.

Vanilla. Rain. Petals.

It clung to him like a second skin.

"You smell like her," I murmured against his neck.

Rook shuddered. A full-body tremor that vibrated into me. "Don't."

"You have her all over you." I dragged my hand down his chest, flattened my palm over his stomach. "Did you like it? Scaring something that helpless?"

Rook turned in my arms. He looked wild. Deranged. "I loved it. I wanted to put her in my pocket. I wanted to bite her."

He grabbed my face between his hands. His palms were rough, calloused from the stick, warm from his blood. He stared at my mouth.

"Taste it," he demanded.

He didn't wait for permission. He crashed his mouth against mine.

It wasn't a soft kiss. Rook didn't do soft. He kissed like he played—violent, chaotic, looking for a weakness. I opened for him instantly, my tongue meeting his, wrestling for dominance.

But the flavor changed everything.

Sweetness.

It was faint, a ghost of a taste transferred from her lips to his, but it hit my tongue like a narcotic. My brain short-circuited. The aggression drained out of me, replaced by a heavy, syrupy need. I groaned, dragging him closer, my hands fisting in the back of his shirt.

Little sugar cube. The thought whispered through my mind. *My tiny, precious thing.*

I tasted her fear on him. I tasted her submission.

I broke the kiss, gasping. We stood forehead to forehead, our breathing harsh and ragged in the quiet apartment.

"You taste like a girl," I accused, my voice rough.

"I know," Rook panted. His eyes were glassy. "It's awful. I want more."

He stepped back, stumbling slightly. He looked down at himself. "I need to... I need to get this out. It hurts."

He started undoing his belt. His hands were shaking so badly he fumbled the buckle.

"Bedroom," I said. "Don't finish without me."

We didn't run, but we didn't walk. We moved with urgent, singular purpose.

The bedroom was vast, dominated by a California King bed with black sheets. We didn't bother with the lights. The city glow bleeding through the windows was enough.

Rook didn't strip. He just shoved his trousers and briefs down to his ankles, kicking them off with a frantic coordination. He fell onto the bed, sprawling on his back. He was glorious—six-foot-six of scarred, hockey-honed muscle, his chest heaving, his cock thick and angry against his stomach.

I followed him. I kept my shirt on, needing the restriction, but I shucked my pants. I climbed onto the bed, positioning myself beside him.

Usually, we touched each other. I would take him in my hand, or he would use his mouth.

Not tonight. Tonight, the ghost of the girl lay between us.

Rook wrapped his hand around himself. He started to stroke, a fast, punishing rhythm. His head fell back against the pillow, his throat exposing the thick cords of muscle working there.

"Talk to me," I ordered. I lay on my side, propped up on an elbow, watching him. I took myself in hand, matching his pace. The friction was good. Grounding. But I needed the mental image. "Tell me what she felt like."

"Small," Rook choked out. His hips bucked off the mattress. "So fucking small, Mercer. My hand... it covered her whole head. I could have snapped her neck by accident."

"But you didn't," I said. A dark satisfaction coiled in my gut. "You were gentle."

"I had to be," he wheezed. "She's made of glass. If I squeezed... she'd shatter."

"Delicate," I supplied. The word made my pulse hammer. "A little trinket."

"Soft," Rook moaned. "Her mouth... it was so soft. No stubble. No resistance. Just... gave way."

I closed my eyes. I pictured it. Not the wet, drowned rat I'd seen, but the creature she really was. A biology student. A nerd. Someone who rescued stray cats in a storm. She was a prey animal. A rabbit. And rabbits needed wolves to keep them safe.

I stroked myself harder, my grip tight. "She was looking at me, Rook."

Rook turned his head on the pillow, watching me. His eyes were heavy-lidded, drugged with lust. "Yeah?"

"When I touched her face," I said, my voice dropping to a devout whisper. "She leaned into it. She wanted me to own her. She has no survival instinct. None."

"Stupid girl," Rook agreed, a fond, twisted smile touching his lips. "Dumb little mouse."

"She needs a keeper," I said. The realization hit me with the force of a slapshot. It wasn't just a want. It was a necessity. A mandate. "Someone to tell her when to eat. When to sleep. When to come."

"Us," Rook grunted. His pace increased. "Has to be us. No one else."

"No one else," I snarled. The thought of another man touching her—some soft-handed college boy who didn't understand the gravity of her fragility—made red spots dance in my vision. "They'd break her. They wouldn't appreciate her."

"We'd keep her safe," Rook panted. "In a cage. A nice cage. With velvet."

"Silk," I corrected. "She likes soft things."

The image destroyed me. Mina, curled up in the center of this massive bed. A tiny spot of white in a sea of black. Her blonde hair spilled over our pillows. My mark on her neck. Rook's mark on her thigh.

"Mina," I whispered.

Rook groaned at the name. "Mercer, I'm close."

"Say it," I commanded. "Say her name."

"Mina," Rook cried out. "Mina. Sweet. Little. Saint."

He arched his back. A guttural shout tore from his throat as he came, his release messy and abundant, coating his hand and stomach.

The sight of his unraveling pushed me over the edge. I imagined spilling inside her, filling that tiny, precious body until she was full of nothing but us.

I shouted, my own release hitting me hard, dragging me under.

For a long time, the only sound in the room was our ragged breathing. The smell of sex mingled with the lingering scent of rain and vanilla that still haunted the air.

Rook dropped his arm over his eyes. His chest rose and fell like a bellows.

I lay back, staring at the ceiling. My heart rate slowed, but the obsession didn't fade. It hardened. It calcified into something permanent.

"We have a problem," Rook said into the darkness, his voice rough.

"I know," I said.

He moved his arm, turning to look at me. The chaos was gone from his eyes, replaced by a terrifying clarity. "I'm not done with her."

"Neither am I."

I reached out, wiping a bead of sweat from his forehead. The intimacy was easy again. The friction was gone. We were aligned.

"She's a distraction," I said, trying one last time to appeal to logic. "We have the playoffs. We have the team."

"Don't care," Rook said flatly. "I want my pet."

I sighed, accepting the inevitable. The data points had shifted. The trajectory was set.

"She's a student," I said, my mind already working through the logistics. Schedules. Locations. Vulnerabilities. "Biology. She'll be at the rink for the tutoring program on Tuesday."

Rook's grin returned. It wasn't the manic, dangerous grin from the hallway. It was slower. Heavier. "Tuesday."

"We don't scare her away next time," I instructed. "We lure her."

"Treats?" Rook suggested.

"Patience," I corrected, though the word tasted like ash. I didn't have patience. I had hunger. "We show her that the monsters can be well-behaved."

"And then?"

I looked at Rook. I looked at the drying mess on his stomach, wasted seed that should have been used to claim her.

"And then," I said, "we take her home and keep her."

Chapter Three

TASTING THE EXCEPTION

POV: Mercer

Logic was a fortress. It was built from stone, reinforced with steel, and patrolled by the ruthless enforcement of cause and effect. I lived in that fortress. I understood the structural integrity of my own existence.

I was a gay man. I was exclusive to Rook. I required hardness, abrasion, and the violent friction of a partner who could take a hit and return it with interest.

The girl was none of those things.

Mina was a structural failure. A soft, crumbling edge in a world of sharp angles.

By all metrics, she should have been invisible to me. A static variable in the background of the arena. Yet, for forty-eight hours, she had been a persistent error code in my operating system.

I stood on the mezzanine level, overlooking the practice rink. The ice was fresh, a sheet of white glass waiting to be scarred by steel blades. It was Tuesday. The rookies were down in the conference room, trudging through their mandatory tutoring sessions.

Rook was currently in the weight room, destroying a punching bag. I could feel his restlessness through our shared connection, a low-grade hum of anxiety that mirrored my own. We hadn't touched each other properly in two days. The sex had been functional, stripping the tension but failing to satisfy the hunger.

Because the hunger had changed.

It was no longer about impact. It was about possession.

"Captain?"

I didn't turn. I knew the tread of the janitorial staff, the heavy stomp of the coaches, and the nervous shuffle of the rookies. This was lighter. Hesitant.

I turned slowly.

Mina stood at the top of the stairs.

She looked ridiculous. She wore an oversized sweater that hung off one shoulder, the knit thick and gray, swallowing her upper body. Her leggings were black, ending at ankles that looked like they would snap if I wrapped a single finger around them. She clutched a stack of biology textbooks against her chest as a shield.

My pulse, usually a slow, resting beat of fifty-five, kicked once. Hard.

"You're late," I lied. She wasn't late. She wasn't even supposed to be seeing me. She was supposed to be in the academic center.

"I... I got lost," she stammered. Her voice was soft, a melodic vibration that grated against my resolve to be cold. "The north corridor is closed for maintenance."

"I closed it," I said.

Her eyes went wide. "Oh."

I stepped away from the railing. The distance between us closed. I moved with deliberate slowness, letting my size do the work. I was six-foot-six in my suit. She was barely five feet of nothing.

"I closed it because I knew you would take the shortcut," I said. "And I wanted you here."

She didn't run. That was the first anomaly. A smart prey animal would have bolted the moment the predator cut off the escape route. Instead, she stood her ground, hugging her books tighter.

Then, she looked at me.

Really looked at me.

Her gaze dropped from my face. It wasn't a polite glance. It was a starving, tactile sweep that felt like wet heat against my skin. She stared at the breadth of my shoulders, her eyes tracing the seam where the suit jacket strained against the deltoids. Her focus drifted lower, lingering on the V of my waistcoat, then down to my hips.

I saw her throat work as she swallowed. Her gaze fixed on my thighs, thick with muscle honed by twenty years of skating, encased in charcoal wool. She looked at me like I was something dense and heavy that she wanted to be crushed under.

It was obscene. It was perfect.

"You're staring," I said, my voice dropping to the register I usually reserved for barking orders on the ice.

A flush stained her cheeks, pink blooming across pale skin. "I... you're very big."

The admission hung in the air, innocent and filthy all at once.

"Yes," I agreed. "And you are absurdly small."

I took another step. I was now inside her personal space. The air shifted. The antiseptic smell of the rink vanished, replaced by that scent.

Vanilla. Rainwater. And something biological—pheromones that screamed *compatible.*

My nostrils flared. It hit the back of my throat like a drug. Rook hadn't been exaggerating. If anything, he had understated the potency. It triggered a primitive, lizard-brain response that bypassed my sexuality entirely and went straight to ownership.

Mine.

The word echoed in the empty mezzanine. *Not for breeding. For keeping.*

"Did you finish with the rookies?" I asked. I needed to keep talking. If I stopped talking, I was going to do something that would ruin my career.

"Yes," she whispered. She tilted her head back to look at me. Her neck was long, white, and terrifyingly exposed. "They... they're not very good at cellular respiration."

"They're paid to hit people, not understand mitochondria," I said. I reached out.

Her breath hitched, a sharp intake of air that sounded loud in the quiet space.

My hand hovered near her face. I remembered the mud. I remembered the texture of her skin under my thumb. I wanted to verify the data.

I brushed my knuckles against her jawline.

Softness.

It was sickening. It was like touching silk stretched over warm water. There was no resistance, no stubble, no grit. Just yielding, feminine heat.

"Rook is losing his mind," I told her, my fingers trailing down to her throat. I felt her pulse hammering there, a frantic bird trapping itself against my touch. "He can't focus. He breaks things. He smells you on his own hands and it makes him mean."

"I didn't mean to," she gasped. Her eyes fluttered shut. She leaned into my hand.

She leaned into it.

The surrender broke me.

"You did," I murmured. "You exist. That's provocation enough."

I stepped closer, pinning her between my body and the cold concrete wall of the mezzanine. I didn't touch her with my body—not yet. I loomed. I let my shadow swallow her whole.

"Rook tasted you," I said. The jealousy was a hot coal in my gut. "He said you tasted like sugar."

Her eyes snapped open. They were gray, the color of a winter sky. "He... he surprised me."

"He's a brute," I said dismissively. "He has no control. He takes what he wants and worries about the consequences later."

"And you?" she asked. The question was barely audible.

"I calculate," I said. "I assess the risk."

I slid my hand to the back of her neck. My fingers tangled in the blonde hair at the base of her skull. It was fine, soft as down. I gripped her, not hard enough to hurt, but firm enough to hold her in place.

"The risk is high," I informed her. "If I kiss you, I confirm the hypothesis. If I confirm the hypothesis, I can't let you go."

Mina didn't pull away. She dropped her books.

They hit the floor with a heavy *thud*, the sound echoing like a gavel strike. Her hands, now empty, reached out. She grabbed the lapels of my jacket. Her fists were tiny, clutching the expensive fabric.

"Confirm it," she challenged.

The audacity. The absolute, reckless stupidity of this creature.

My control snapped.

I didn't crash into her like Rook. I descended. I lowered my head, watching her eyes until the very last second, until I saw the anticipation dilate her pupils.

I pressed my mouth to hers.

I expected it to be awful. I expected the texture to be wrong, the shape to be alien. I expected to recoil from the femininity of it.

I didn't.

She was soft, yes. But she was hot. Her mouth opened under mine with a desperate, eager compliance that made my knees weak.

Then the taste hit me.

It wasn't just sugar. It was warmth. It was a biological connection that felt like plugging into a high-voltage socket. It seared through my veins, lighting up nerve endings I didn't know I possessed. It was a sweetness that didn't cloy; it addicted.

I groaned, a low, guttural sound that vibrated against her lips. I deepened the kiss, tilting her head back, demanding access.

She gave it. She gave everything. Her tongue met mine, shy and uncertain, and the contact sent a shockwave straight to my groin. I hardened instantly, painfully, the blood rushing south with a violence that made my head spin.

Soft, my brain screamed. *She is the soft place.*

I needed more. I shifted, pressing my hips against hers. The size difference was laughable. I could feel her small, curved stomach against the hard ridge of my erection. She felt fragile, like I could crush her effortlessly, and that fragility called to the monster inside me. The part of me that wanted to protect, to hoard, to keep safe.

I swept my tongue into her mouth, exploring the ridges of her teeth, the slick heat of her palate. I tasted the coffee she'd had earlier. I tasted her want.

She made a noise—a high, mewling sound in the back of her throat.

It destroyed me.

I pulled back, just an inch, gasping for air. We were both breathing heavy, the sound ragged in the quiet space.

Her lips were red, swollen from my attention. Her eyes were glazed, unfocused. She looked thoroughly, beautifully wrecked.

"Rook was right," I whispered, my voice sounding like it had been dragged over broken glass. "You taste like ruin."

Mina blinked, trying to focus on my face. Her hands were still clutching my lapels, anchoring her to me.

"Are you... are you going to let me go?" she asked.

I stared down at her. I looked at the way her hair was messed up from my grip. I looked at the wet sheen on her lips. I looked at the way she fit into the shadow of my body as if she had been engineered for that exact purpose.

I ran the calculation again.

Variables: Two volatile, possessive men. One fragile, intoxicating woman.

Outcome: Catastrophic failure of all previous boundaries.

"No," I said. "I'm not letting you go."

I grabbed her wrist. My fingers wrapped all the way around, overlapping easily.

"Where are we going?" she asked, stumbling as I turned, pulling her with me.

"To find Rook," I said. "He's waiting in the car."

"But... my books."

I didn't look back at the pile on the floor.

"You don't need books," I told her, dragging her toward the exit. "You need to learn a different subject today."

The fortress of logic hadn't fallen. It had just been repurposed. It was no longer a defense against the world. It was a cage. And I had just caught the only thing worth keeping inside it.

Chapter Four

The Impossible Instinct

POV: Mina

The microscope slide was cold against her fingertips, a sharp contrast to the phantom heat still burning the back of her neck.

Two days. It had been two days since the gala, since she'd walked up to the NHL's twin pillars of violence and been reduced to ash with a single, synchronized sneer.

Mina adjusted the lens, desperate to drown in the cellular structures, but the circle of light magnified nothing but her own unraveling. The *Paramecium* moved with simple, predictable cilia strokes. Eat. Divide. Exist.

Her own biology was revoltingly complex.

A tremor worked its way through her hand, vibrating down the metal shaft of the adjustment knob. She pulled her fingers back, curling them into her palm. Her skin felt too tight, stretched over her bones like a drumhead waiting to be struck.

Withdrawal.

The diagnosis hit her with clinical detachment, though the symptoms were messy and wet. She was suffering from withdrawal. Not from a substance, but from a proximity.

Since Sunday night, her body had rejected homeostasis. She couldn't regulate her temperature; flashes of feverish heat alternated with bone-deep chills that had nothing to do with the campus AC. Food tasted like cardboard. Sleep was a fever dream of heavy hands and blue eyes that looked at her with the terrifying, gentle focus of a wolf deciding which bone to break first.

"Mina? You okay?"

The voice came from the next station. Kevin. A nice, safe, average-sized doctoral candidate with soft hands and a penchant for argyle sweaters.

Mina flinched. The sound of her name in his voice grated on her nerves like sandpaper. It was too high. Too polite. It lacked the subsonic rumble that vibrated in the hollow of a chest cavity.

"I'm fine," she said. Her voice sounded thin, brittle. "Just tired."

Kevin stepped closer. He smelled of fabric softener and stale coffee. It was a benign scent. A human scent.

It made her stomach turn.

"You've been staring at that slide for twenty minutes without taking a note," Kevin pointed out, offering a hesitant smile. He reached out, his hand hovering near her shoulder. "You look a little pale."

His palm landed on her deltoid.

The reaction was instantaneous and violent.

Mina's skin crawled. A wave of repulsion rolled through her gut, so potent she nearly gagged. His touch felt clammy, weak, utterly *wrong*. It wasn't heavy enough. It didn't possess the devastating gravity that anchored a person to the earth. It was a moth fluttering against a windowpane, annoying and insignificant.

She jerked away, her stool screeching against the linoleum.

Kevin recoiled, holding his hands up. "Whoa. Sorry. Just checking on you."

Mina breathed through her mouth, trying to scrub the sensation of his normalcy from her skin. "Don't," she snapped, the aggression foreign on her tongue. "Just... don't touch me."

Kevin blinked, hurt flashing in his eyes. "Right. Okay. Sorry."

He retreated to his side of the lab, muttering something about stress.

Mina gripped the edge of the slate table. Her breathing came in short, jagged gasps.

Defective. She was defective.

She closed her eyes, and immediately, the memory assaulted her.

Rook. The chaotic, beautiful disaster. The smell of scotch and rain. The way he had crowded her into that alcove, blocking out the light, consuming the oxygen. He hadn't asked. He had taken. And her body, her traitorous, instinct-driven body, hadn't fought him. It had sung.

And *Mercer*.

The memory of the Captain was different. It was slower. Heavier.

She lifted a trembling hand to her cheek. She could still feel the ghost of his thumb. Rough, calloused skin dragging through the mud on her face. He had looked at her not with lust—lust was common, cheap—but with a terrifying species of possessiveness. He had cleaned her. He had inspected her.

The adults are talking inside. The nursery is closed.

He spoke to her like she was a child, a pet, something too fragile for the world he inhabited. And God help her, she wanted to be that thing. She wanted to be the small, precious object he tucked inside his jacket, safe from the storm, just like that kitten.

The ache between her legs pulsed, a heavy, wet throb that made sitting uncomfortable.

She needed them.

It was a biological imperative, bypassing logic, bypassing pride. It was the MHC compatibility theory gone nuclear. Her genetic code had scanned them, identified the apex predators, and rewritten her survival instincts to align with their dominance.

She checked the clock on the wall.

1:45 PM. Tuesday.

The tutoring session with the rookies started at 2:30 PM.

She shouldn't go.

Logic dictated she call in sick. She should go back to her dorm, lock the door, and bury herself under a weighted blanket until this madness passed. Going back to the arena was walking into the lion's den wearing a steak necklace. They had told her to run. Mercer had explicitly ordered her to flee before they changed their minds.

A dark, syrupy heat pooled in her belly at the thought of them changing their minds.

What did that look like? If *run* was the mercy, what was the alternative?

Mina stood up. Her legs felt shaky, but her movements were decisive. She packed her notes. She shoved the textbook into her bag.

She wasn't going to the dorm.

She was going to the slaughter.

*

The employee entrance of the arena was a steel maw that swallowed the afternoon sun.

Mina flashed her badge at the security guard—an older man named Frank who usually gave her a grandfatherly wink. Today, she barely saw him. Her vision tunnelled.

The air inside the stadium was different. It was recycled, filtered, and kept at a crisp sixty degrees, but beneath the artificial chill lay the scent of the ice. It was a sharp, mineral tang that coated the back of the throat.

And beneath that... *them*.

It was impossibly faint, likely a psychosomatic hallucination, but as she walked down the long concrete corridor toward the academic center, she swore she could smell sandalwood and ozone.

Her body reacted before her brain caught up. Her nipples hardened against the scratchy wool of her oversized sweater. The fabric was a shield, a gray fortress she'd constructed to hide the soft curves they had inspected with such disdain. She had worn her oldest leggings, unauthorized sneakers, and no makeup. She tried to look like the "drowned rat" Mercer had named her.

If she looked pathetic enough, maybe they would ignore her.

Liar, her inner voice whispered. *You hope they eat you.*

She reached the junction where the hallway split. To the left, the main concourse. To the right, the shortcut past the practice rink that led to the classrooms.

A yellow folding sign blocked the right corridor. *MAINTENANCE. NO ENTRY.*

Mina paused. The detour would add ten minutes. She would be late. Mercer—if he even cared about the tutoring program—hated lateness. He ran the team with the precision of a Swiss watch.

She looked at the sign. There was no noise of construction. No workers. Just the quiet hum of the building.

She chewed her lip. A bad habit. She tasted the copper where the skin had split two days ago. Rook's mark.

She stepped around the sign.

The corridor was dim. The overhead fluorescents were powered down to energy-saving mode, leaving pools of shadow between the lights. Her sneakers squeaked on the polished concrete.

Squeak. Squeak. Like a mouse.

The metaphor was too accurate. She was scurrying through the walls of their castle.

She reached the mezzanine stairs. The practice rink lay below, a vast sheet of white perfection.

She stopped.

The silence was absolute. No pucks hitting the glass. No skates carving the ice. Just the heavy, waiting stillness of a predator holding its breath.

She walked to the railing. She couldn't help herself. She needed to look.

The ice was empty.

Disappointment crashed into her, heavy and suffocating. She gripped the cold metal rail, her knuckles turning white. They weren't here. Of course they weren't here. They were professionals. They had lives, media appearances, people who didn't look like drowned rats to attend to.

She was just a biology student with a glandular problem.

"You're late."

The voice didn't come from the ice. It came from behind her.

It was a low, resonant baritone that bypassed her auditory nerves and vibrated directly against her spine. It was the sound of a closing door. The sound of a sentence being passed.

Mina froze.

Her heart didn't hammer; it seized. A wet, heavy heat flooded her veins, turning her blood to molten lead.

She knew that voice. She had replayed it in her head a thousand times in the last forty-eight hours. It was the voice that had called her *pathetic*.

Slowly, terrifyingly slowly, she turned.

Mercer stood at the top of the stairs she had just descended.

He blocked the exit. He blocked the light.

He was massive. In the dim hallway, he looked less like a man and more like a monolith carved from granite and resentment. He wasn't wearing his gear. He was in a navy suit today, the jacket cut to accommodate the violent width of his shoulders, the waistcoat straining against a chest that rose and fell with a steady, hypnotic rhythm.

He watched her.

There was no disdain in his eyes today. The ice-blue irises were dark, the pupils blown so wide they looked like black coins. He looked at her with a terrifying, blank intensity. It was the look a scientist gave a new specimen. Or a starving man gave a loaf of bread.

He took a step down. Then another.

The heavy *thud* of his dress shoes on the metal stairs echoed in the empty mezzanine.

Thud.

Thud.

Mina couldn't move. Her feet were nailed to the floor. Her flight response had short-circuited, replaced entirely by the *freeze* and *submit* protocols.

"I... I got lost," she lied. Her voice was a wisp of smoke. "The sign..."

"I put it there," Mercer said.

He reached the landing. He loomed over her, sucking the air out of the space. He smelled of control. He smelled of the very thing she had been withdrawing from.

The relief was dizzying. It washed over her, making her knees weak. He was here. He was real. He was looking at her.

"Why?" she whispered.

Mercer didn't answer immediately. He invaded her personal space, collapsing the distance until she had to crane her neck back to look him in the eye. He studied her face, his gaze tracing the dark circles under her eyes, the pallor of her cheeks, the tremble of her lower lip.

"You look terrible," he said softly.

It sounded like a compliment. It sounded like *worship*.

"I haven't... I haven't been sleeping well," Mina admitted. The truth tumbled out. She couldn't lie to him. It felt like lying to gravity.

"Good," Mercer murmured. A muscle feathered in his jaw. "Neither have we."

He raised a hand.

Mina stopped breathing. The air trapped in her lungs burned.

He didn't strike her. He didn't grab her. He reached out and touched the loose, hanging collar of her oversized sweater. His fingers were thick, scarred, and overwhelmingly masculine against the grey wool. He rubbed the fabric between his thumb and forefinger, testing the texture.

"Hiding?" he asked. His knuckles brushed the sensitive skin of her collarbone.

A jolt of electricity arced through her, so intense her vision blurred. She swayed forward, magnetized.

"I'm cold," she stammered.

"You're not cold," Mercer corrected. His voice dropped to a rough purr. "You're waiting."

He stepped closer. His thighs brushed hers. Hard wool against soft leggings. Rock against water.

"Rook is in the car," Mercer said, his gaze dropping to her mouth. "He's vibrating. He wanted to come up here and throw you over his shoulder. He lacks patience."

"And you?" Mina breathed.

"I have patience," Mercer lied. She could see the lie in the tension of his neck, in the way his other hand opened and closed at his side, grasping at empty air as if he wanted to strangle something. Or hold something very tight. "I wanted to see if you came back."

He slid his hand from her sweater to her neck. His palm was hot, dry, and enormous. It cupped the nape of her neck, his fingers wrapping around to her throat. He could crush her windpipe with a twitch.

Instead, his thumb stroked the pulse point under her jaw. It was fluttering like a trapped bird.

"You came back," he whispered, sounding almost disappointed. Almost resigned. "Stupid little thing. You walked right back into the trap."

"I had to," Mina confessed. Tears pricked her eyes—not from sadness, but from the overwhelming pressure of his presence. "I couldn't stay away."

Mercer's eyes darkened. The black holes of his pupils swallowed the blue.

"Biology," he diagnosed. "A glitch."

"Yes."

"Does it hurt?" he asked. He pressed his thumb harder against her pulse, stealing her breath for a second.

"Yes," she gasped when he released the pressure. "It hurts all the time."

"Good."

Mercer leaned down. His face was inches from hers. She could feel the heat radiating off him, a furnace contained within a suit.

"We tried to purge it," he told her, his voice a secret shared in the dark. "We tried to scrub you off. Rook scrubbed until his skin was red. I tried to focus on the game. On him."

He paused, his nose brushing against hers. He inhaled sharply, dragging her scent into his lungs.

"It didn't work," he said. "You're a contagion, Mina. And we're sick."

He didn't wait for permission. He didn't ask if she wanted this. He simply accepted the reality of her submission.

His mouth descended on hers.

Mina whimpered, her hands flying up to clutch his lapels. It wasn't the chaotic assault Rook had delivered. This was a siege. Mercer's lips were firm, commanding, and devastatingly skilled. He kissed her with a terrifying precision, molding her mouth to his, tasting her with a thoroughness that suggested he was memorizing her genetic sequence.

She melted.

There was no other word for it. Her bones turned to liquid. The tension that had plagued her for forty-eight hours evaporated, replaced by a heavy, golden surrender. She opened for him, inviting him in, desperate to be filled by his taste.

He tasted of mint and dark, repressed hunger.

He groaned, a low sound that vibrated against her lips, and pulled her body flush against his. The evidence of his own "sickness" pressed hard against her stomach. He was aroused. The great, icy Captain was hard for her.

The realization shattered the last of her rational mind.

Mine, the beast in her chest purred. *The monsters are mine.*

Mercer broke the kiss, breathless. His forehead rested against hers. His hands were gripping her arms now, holding her up because her legs had ceased to function.

"You don't need those books," he rasped, looking down at the bag slipping from her shoulder.

"I..." Mina blinked, dazed. "My students..."

"Gone," Mercer said. "Dismissed. You have a new lesson."

He turned her toward the exit, his arm wrapping around her waist like an iron band. He didn't push; he carried her weight, absorbing her into his side.

"Where?" she asked, stumbling as she tried to match his long strides.

"To the car," Mercer said. "To Rook."

He looked down at her, his expression grim, possessive, and terrifyingly gentle.

"We're taking you home," he stated. "And we're going to fix this."

Mina didn't ask how. She didn't care. As they walked toward the exit, leaving her textbooks on the floor of the mezzanine, she knew only one thing.

The withdrawal was over. The overdose was about to begin.

Chapter Five

No Space for Denial

POV: Mina

The air in the equipment archive tasted of rubber, stale ice, and the ozone charge of a coming storm. It was a dead, chemical smell, heavy in lungs that refused to expand fully.

Mina stumbled as the heavy steel door slammed shut behind her, the sound vibrating through the soles of her wet sneakers. The lock engaged with a definitive, mechanical *thunk* that echoed in the marrow of her bones.

Silence followed. Absolute, heavy, and suffocating.

She stood in the sudden gloom, the only light bleeding in from a high, barred window where hail was already beginning to hammer against the glass. The room was a graveyard of athletic violence—stacks of black pucks like monoliths, rows of taped sticks leaning against the concrete walls like spears, and racks of jerseys hanging like ghosts.

But the room wasn't empty.

Rook waited in the center of the concrete floor.

He was pacing, a tiger in a cage too small for its ambition. He wore only his practice joggers, low on his hips, the strings untied and hanging loose. His chest was bare, a vast landscape of scarred, tanned muscle that seemed to suck the remaining light from the room. Sweat sheened his skin, making him glisten like he'd just been birthed from something primal.

He stopped moving the moment the door sealed.

His head snapped toward her. Dark curls, damp with sweat, fell over eyes that burned with a chaotic, frenzied intelligence. He didn't look at Mercer. He looked at her.

And then he smiled.

It wasn't a nice smile. It was a baring of teeth, a terrifying expression of relief that bordered on madness.

"You brought it," Rook breathed. His voice was a rasp, a sound that bypassed her ears and vibrated directly in her pelvic floor.

"She walked right into the trap," Mercer said from behind her.

His hand was still on the nape of her neck, his thumb pressing into the soft indentation of her spine. He didn't push her forward. He held her there, a possessive anchor preventing her from bolting, though there was nowhere to run.

"Is she real?" Rook took a step forward. "She looks like a hallucination. A wet, shivering little ghost."

"She's real," Mercer confirmed. His thumb stroked her skin, a slow, rhythmic motion that felt obscenely intimate. "And she's freezing."

Mina trembled. It wasn't just the cold rain that had soaked through her oversized sweater. It was the biological alarm blaring in her hindbrain. *Predators. Apex. Run.* But the signal was getting jammed by a louder, wetter frequency. *Submit. Stay. Belong.*

"I'm... I'm not a ghost," she managed to whisper. Her voice sounded thin, fractured against the hard surfaces of the room.

Rook let out a noise that was half-laugh, half-growl. He closed the distance between them in two long, stalking strides. He was so big. Up close, the scale of him was nonsensical. He blocked out the room, the world, the logic of physics. He was a wall of heat and scent—sandalwood, musk, and the sharp tang of copper.

He dropped to his knees.

The movement was so sudden, so fluid, that Mina flinched back against Mercer's chest.

Mercer didn't let her retreat. His other hand came around her waist, a band of steel clamping her to his front. "Stay," he ordered, his voice vibrating against her ear. "Let him look."

Rook wasn't looking at her face. He was looking at her legs.

He reached out, his hands massive, scarred from a thousand fights on the ice. He didn't grab. He touched the hem of her soaked leggings with a reverence that made her stomach flip.

"So small," Rook murmured. He sounded devastated. "Look at this, Merc. Her ankles. I could snap them with two fingers."

"Don't confirm the structural weakness," Mercer scolded gently, as if training a particularly large, dangerous dog. "You'll scare her."

"I don't want to break her," Rook whispered, looking up at Mina with eyes that were wide and glassy. "I want to put her in a jar. I want to keep the dust off her."

He pressed his face against her knee.

The contact seared through the wet fabric. His cheek was hot, rough with stubble. He inhaled deeply, dragging the scent of damp cotton and her own terror into his lungs.

"Sugar," he groaned. "She still smells like sugar. Even under the rain."

Mina's knees buckled.

Mercer caught her instantly. He lifted her effortlessly, her feet leaving the floor as he adjusted his grip, holding her suspended against his chest.

"The storm," Mercer said to Rook. "The lockdown protocols just engaged. We're stuck."

Rook stood up. He loomed over them both now, his height terrifying. "Stuck? With her?"

"For hours, likely."

Rook's gaze drifted over Mina's face. He looked at her wet lashes, her parted lips, the flush spreading down her neck. "Good. She needs drying."

"Put me down," Mina squeaked. "Please. I have... I have class."

"Cancelled," Mercer said against her temple. "The university is closed for the weather. The roads are closed. The world stops for the storm, little mouse. Which means you belong to the room now."

He walked her further into the space, toward a large, padded equipment bench pushed against the far wall. He sat down heavily, pulling her onto his lap.

She sat straddling his thigh, her legs dangling uselessly. She felt like a doll. A toy he had picked up and decided to keep.

Rook followed. He didn't give them space. He crowded in, dropping to sit on the bench beside Mercer, his thigh pressing hard against Mina's side.

She was bracketed. Wall of muscle to her left. Wall of muscle beneath her.

"She's shaking," Rook noted. He reached out and touched her wet sweater. "Take this off. She'll get pneumonia. A sick pet is a useless pet."

"I'm not a pet," Mina protested, though her hands were clutching Mercer's lapels, seeking stability in the earthquake of their presence.

"Shh," Mercer soothed. It was a terrifying sound—a low, rumbling purr. He began to unbutton his suit jacket. "You don't get to decide what you are right now. Your biology decided for you when you walked in here. You're the soft thing. We are the hard things. That is the taxonomy."

He shed his jacket. Then his vest. Underneath, his white dress shirt was crisp, straining against the dense muscle of his chest.

"Rook is right," Mercer said. "The wet clothes go."

Mina's heart slammed against her ribs. "I'm not naked underneath. I mean... I am, but..."

"We know what anatomy is, Mina," Rook drawled. He leaned in, his nose brushing her ear. "We've seen plenty of girls. Never wanted to touch one before. They're usually... loud. Complicated."

"Sharp," Mercer added. "You're not sharp. You're round."

Mercer's hands went to the hem of her sweater.

"Wait," Mina gasped, clamping her elbows to her sides. "You're gay. You... you don't do this."

Mercer paused. He looked at Rook. A silent communication passed between them—a shared frequency of obsession.

"We don't do women," Mercer corrected. He leaned forward, touching his forehead to hers. His blue eyes were endless, freezing oceans. "We don't want women, Mina. We want *you*. It's a very specific distinction."

"You're the exception," Rook whispered, his fingers dancing along her spine through the wet wool. "The glitch. The little pink error code in our programming."

"And we're going to debug you," Mercer finished.

He pulled the sweater up.

Mina didn't fight. She couldn't. Her arms lifted of their own accord, betraying her. The wet wool peeled away, leaving her in a thin, lace tank top that offered zero protection against the chill or their gazes.

The air hit her damp skin, raising gooseflesh instantly.

Rook hissed. The sound was sharp, pained. "Look at her skin, Merc. It's so white. It's practically translucent."

He reached out. His hand was trembling. He traced the line of her collarbone with one thick finger.

"Porcelain," Rook whispered. "If I bite her, she'll bruise purple. Like a plum."

"Control yourself," Mercer warned, though his own hand flattened against her bare back, his palm a scorching brand. "We need to warm her up."

"Body heat," Rook suggested. The predatory glint in his eye darkened. "Thermodynamics."

"Effective," Mercer agreed.

"Come here," Rook said.

He didn't wait. He grabbed Mina by the waist and hauled her off Mercer's lap and onto his own.

The transition was jarring. Mercer was hard, like sitting on a statue. Rook was hard, but he vibrated. His energy hummed against her thighs. He wrapped his arms around her, burying his face in the crook of her neck.

"Mine for a minute," Rook growled into her skin. "You had her on the stairs."

"Share," Mercer commanded.

Rook groaned but didn't argue. He pulled Mina back until her spine rested against his bare chest. He was a radiator. The heat coming off him was immense. He wrapped his massive arms around her, crossing them over her chest, effectively locking her in a cage of bone and muscle.

Mercer didn't move away. He shifted closer on the bench, turning so his knee pressed between hers, forcing her legs apart.

Mina whimpered. The position was obscene. She was sprawled across the Enforcer, held captive by his limbs, while the Captain invaded the space between her thighs.

"Better?" Mercer asked softly. He reached out and cupped her face. His thumb brushed over her cheekbone.

"I..." Mina's brain misfired. "I'm warm."

"Good." Mercer's gaze dropped to her mouth. "Because you were turning blue. And we can't have our little prize damaged by the weather."

"Why?" Mina asked. The question tore out of her. "Why me? I'm nothing. I'm clumsy. I'm awkward. I smell like chemicals half the time."

Rook tightened his hold, his nose dragging along her jawline. "You smell like peace," he mumbled. "Like the quiet part of the noise."

Mercer leaned in. "Do you know what it's like for us, Mina? Every day?"

She shook her head, the movement limited by Rook's grip.

"It's loud," Mercer said. "Aggression. Expectation. The constant, grinding friction of being at the top of the food chain. Rook and I... we sharpened each other until there was nothing left but edges. We cut everything we touch."

He ran his thumb over her lower lip, pulling it down to expose the wet pink inside.

"But you," he whispered. "You're soft. You force us to be careful. It's the only time we get to stop fighting. To protect you, we have to stop trying to destroy everything else."

"You're a pacifier," Rook said bluntly against her ear. "A stress toy. But... pretty. And sweet."

"Sickeningly sweet," Mercer agreed.

He moved his hand from her face down to her neck, then lower. His palm covered her heart. He could feel it hammering, a frantic drum solo against her ribs.

"Your heart is going to explode," Mercer noted clinically.

"You're terrifying," Mina gasped.

"We know," they said in unison.

Rook's hand moved. One of his large palms slid from her stomach up to cup her breast through the thin lace.

Mina jolted. A bolt of lightning shot straight to her groin.

"Rook," Mercer warned.

"Checking for warmth," Rook lied. He squeezed. Not hard. Just enough to weigh the flesh in his hand, to measure the softness against his calloused palm. "God. She's so..."

"She's not a stress ball, Rook," Mercer said, though he didn't stop him. "Be gentle."

"I am being gentle," Rook insisted. "I'm barely touching her. Look."

He used his thumb to brush over the peak of her breast. The nipple hardened instantly, peaking against the lace.

Mina bit her lip to swallow a moan. It didn't work. The sound escaped, a small, pathetic mewl.

The sound changed the atmosphere in the room instantly.

Mercer's eyes flared. His pupils swallowed the blue completely. The analytical coldness fractured, revealing the monster beneath.

"She likes it," Mercer observed. His voice was thick.

"Of course she likes it," Rook growled. He bit the sensitive cord of her neck, a grazing of teeth that was more claim than injury. "She's ours. Her body knows it even if her brain is too stupid to catch up."

"Is that true, little mouse?" Mercer asked.

He moved his hand from her chest, sliding it down her torso, over the waistband of her leggings, and rested it heavily on the apex of her thighs.

Mina stopped breathing. The heat of his hand burned through the fabric.

"Does your body know who owns it?" Mercer demanded.

Mina looked at him. She looked at the severe lines of his face, the beautiful, cruel mouth that had kissed her into oblivion on the stairs. She felt the massive, vibrating energy of Rook behind her, his heart beating against her back like a war drum.

They were monsters. They were gay men who had somehow rewired their entire existence to accommodate her softness. They wanted to keep her in a jar. They wanted to own her.

And the empty, aching void inside her—the loneliness that had followed her through labs and libraries—snapped shut.

"Yes," she whispered.

Mercer smiled.

It wasn't the polite smile he gave donors. It was a terrifying, beautiful expression of absolute victory.

"Good girl."

He didn't move his hand. He just pressed down. Friction. Pressure.

"The storm raging beyond the glass is going to last a long time," Mercer murmured, his voice a low, vibrating baritone that seemed to resonate in the hollows of her bones. His ice-cold eyes never left hers, pinning her in place more effectively than any shackle. "The aether screams tonight. Rook is bored... and a bored Rook is a dangerous thing. I am stressed. The weight of maintaining order amidst chaos wears on the soul."

He ground the heel of his palm down against her public mound, a deliberate, heavy friction that wrung a shattered, desperate gasp from her throat. The pressure was borderline painful, bruising and perfect, sending a jolt of electricity straight to her core.

"And you..." Mercer's pupils blew wide, swallowing the iris until his eyes were pools of endless black. "You are very, very useful."

Rook shifted behind her, a massive wall of heat and muscle. He buried his face in her neck, inhaling like a predator scenting wounded prey.

Chapter Six

Audience of One

POV: Mercer

The ice was a sheet of black glass reflecting the high, industrial beams of the arena ceiling. It was late. The kind of late where the silence of the city bled through the concrete walls, heavy and muffling. The janitorial staff had long since finished their rounds, the Zamboni was parked in its bay, and the overhead lights were dimmed to a singular, spotlight bank over center ice.

It was just us. Just the scrape of steel on frozen water.

And her.

I didn't need to look up to know exactly where she was. I could feel her presence in the VIP box three levels up like a phantom limb. A magnetic pull in the iron of my blood, dragging my attention upward, away from the puck, away from the game, away from sanity.

Mina.

She was supposed to be studying. We had given her the code to the suite, told her the Wi-Fi was faster than the campus network, told her it was safer than the library at midnight. Lies. Tactical deceptions. We wanted her here because the apartment felt like a tomb without her scent lingering in the hallway. We wanted her here because Rook couldn't sleep unless he knew exactly where she was.

And I... I needed an audience.

"Focus, Cap," Rook growled.

The sound of his skates tearing the ice came before the impact. He hit me low, his shoulder driving into my hip with the force of a battering ram. I absorbed the blow, my skates carving deep gouges into the ice as I pivoted, using his own momentum to spin off the check.

He was fast tonight. Manic.

Rook didn't stop. He turned on a dime, spraying a wave of snow, and came at me again. He wasn't playing the puck. He was hunting. His eyes were wild, dark holes in a face slick with sweat. He was performing.

We both were.

I caught the puck on my blade, the familiar vibration of rubber on carbon fiber grounding me. I accelerated. The wind rushed past my ears, cooling the sweat on my neck. I felt heavy—two hundred and forty pounds of muscle and kinetic energy moving at thirty miles an hour.

Usually, I hated the way I was built. I hated the space I took up, the way chairs creaked under me, the way doorways felt too narrow. My body was a tool for violence, engineered for impact, not for comfort.

But tonight, with her watching, the monstrous size of my frame felt like a purpose.

I glanced up as I rounded the net.

She was there. A small, pale shape pressed against the glass of the luxury box. She wasn't looking at her books. She wasn't looking at her laptop.

She was looking at me.

The sensation of her gaze was physical. It didn't just land on me; it dragged. It felt like warm, wet silk sliding over my skin, heavier than my equipment, hotter than the exertion burning in my lungs.

She was watching my thighs.

I knew it with a sudden, devastating certainty. She was watching the way the muscles in my legs bunched and fired with every stride. She was analyzing the brutal width of my quads, the thick cords of tendon shifting under the socks. To anyone else, I was just a defenseman doing drills. To her, I was a titan.

A dark, sinful pride uncoiled in my chest.

Look at me, little mouse, I thought, pushing harder, digging my edges in until the ice screamed. *Look at the monster. See how strong the walls of your cage are.*

I wanted her to objectify me. I wanted her to reduce me to meat and force. I wanted her to look at my hands—hands that could palm a basketball or crush a throat—and wonder what they would feel like wrapped around her waist.

Rook cut across the center line, intercepting me. He didn't go for the puck this time. He went for the body.

He slammed me into the boards.

The collision was massive. The Plexiglas rattled, a thunderclap that echoed through the empty stadium. Pain flared in my shoulder, sharp and bright, but it was distant. Secondary.

Rook pinned me there. His forearm pressed against my throat, his chest heaving against mine. He smelled of feral exertion and expensive soap.

"She's watching," Rook panted, his voice a wrecked whisper against my ear. "I can feel her eyes on my back. It burns, Merc. It fucking burns."

"I know," I gritted out, shoving back against him.

"Does she like it?" Rook asked, grinding his hips against mine. He was hard. Thickly, painfully hard in his cup. "Does she like seeing us tear each other apart?"

"She loves it," I lied, though I suspected it was the truth. "She's sick. Just like us."

I threw an elbow, catching him in the ribs. He grunted, a wet, breathless laugh escaping him, and backed off.

We began to circle each other.

This wasn't practice. This was a mating dance. Two apex predators showing the female that we could kill anything that came near her. We were displaying our violence like peacock feathers, promising her that the same brutality we used on the ice would be used to keep the world away from her soft skin.

I skated backward, keeping my eyes on Rook, but my awareness remained fixed on the glass three stories up.

I imagined her view.

She would see the width of my shoulders, exaggerated by the pads but undeniably massive underneath. She would see the way the jersey pulled tight across my back when I reached for the puck. She would see the sweat dripping from my chin, the snarl on my face, the absolute, unyielding control I exerted over a surface that made other men fall.

Does she understand the physics of it? The biology?

I am six-foot-six. My resting heart rate is forty-two. I can leg press a small car. And yet, the thought of her—five feet of clumsy softness—makes my hands shake.

I stopped at the blue line and wound up. I didn't aim for the net. I aimed for the glass directly below her suite.

I fired the puck.

It was a slapshot, pure rage and power chanelled through the stick. The puck flew at a hundred miles an hour.

BAM.

It hit the glass high up, dead center below where she stood. The sound was a gunshot.

Above, I saw her jump. She flinched back, her hands flying to her mouth.

"Too loud," Rook criticized, skating up beside me. He leaned on his stick, his chest rising and falling like a bellows. "You scared her."

"I woke her up," I corrected.

I skated to the boards, right below her box. I couldn't see her clearly through the angle of the glass and the reflection of the lights, just the outline of her oversized cardigan and the pale blur of her face.

I took off my helmet.

The cool air hit my wet hair. I wiped the sweat from my eyes with the back of my glove and glared up at her.

Come here.

I didn't say it. I didn't have to. The command radiated off me.

Rook joined me. He didn't bother with silent commands. He slammed his gloved fist against the glass.

"Come down!" he roared, his voice booming through the empty arena. "Bring the books!"

She hesitated. I saw her shrink back slightly, overwhelmed by the volume, by the size of him even from this distance.

"Rook," I warned quietly. "Gentle."

"I am gentle," he argued, looking up at her with a hunger that could swallow the world. "I just want her closer. I can't smell her from here."

I looked up again. She was moving now. She was packing her bag. Not running away. Running *to* us.

My chest tightened. It was a painful, constricting sensation that had nothing to do with the check I'd just taken.

Trust.

That was the weapon she used against us. She trusted us. She had seen us brawl, seen us bleed, heard us snarl, and yet she was coming down the stairs. She looked at two monsters and saw a sanctuary.

It was the most manipulative thing she could possibly do.

If she feared us, we could let her go. Fear was rational. Fear meant she understood the danger.

But this... this blind, biological faith that we wouldn't crush her? It obligated me. It bound me to her with chains of iron. I had to protect her, because she clearly lacked the survival instinct to protect herself.

"She's coming," Rook whispered. He was vibrating. He tapped his stick against the ice, a nervous, rhythmic *tap-tap-tap*.

We waited by the gate where the Zamboni entered.

Minutes ticked by. The anticipation was agony. I could hear my own pulse in my ears, heavy and slow.

Then, the heavy steel door at the end of the tunnel creaked open.

She appeared.

She looked tiny in the cavernous space. She was wearing yellow today—a soft, buttery color that made her look like a patch of sunlight lost in a thunderstorm. Her cardigan hung to her knees, swallowing her hands. She clutched her bag to her chest like a shield.

She stopped at the edge of the rubber matting, ten feet away from the ice.

The air in the arena shifted. The cold, sterile smell of the rink vanished, replaced instantly by that scent. Vanilla. Rain. Warm sugar.

Rook made a noise in his throat—a low, rumbling growl.

"Closer," I ordered. My voice was rough, darker than I intended.

Mina stepped onto the mat. She walked toward the boards, her eyes wide, darting between us. She stopped right at the gate.

We were on skates, which made the height difference comical. We towered over her by nearly two feet. We were armored, sweaty, and violent. She was soft, dry, and clean.

She looked up at me. Her gaze traveled from my skates, up my shin pads, over the hockey pants, past the chest protector, to my face.

She licked her lips.

"You were fighting," she whispered. Her voice trembled, but not with fear. With excitement.

"Training," I corrected. I leaned over the boards, resting my gloved hands on the ledge, looming over her. "Did you watch?"

"I..." She swallowed. "I couldn't look away."

"Good."

"You're big," she blurted out. Her face flushed pink instantly. "I mean... from up there. You look... heavy. Like nothing could move you."

Rook laughed. He skated over, stopping so hard he sprayed snow over the toes of her sneakers.

"He is heavy," Rook agreed. "He's a wall. But I moved him."

"You cheap-shotted me," I said without looking at Rook. My eyes were fixed on Mina. "Did you see my legs, Mina?"

Her blush deepened to a dark crimson. "What?"

"I felt you staring at my legs," I said. I stripped off one glove, dropping it on the ice. I reached over the boards.

My hand was bare, steaming slightly in the cold air. I reached for her face.

She didn't flinch. She leaned in. She met my hand halfway, pressing her cheek into my palm.

The contact was electric. Her skin was impossibly soft, warm, and alive. My thumb brushed her cheekbone, sensing the fragile structure beneath. I could crush it. I could ruin her.

She closed her eyes and let out a soft sigh.

"I was watching your legs," she admitted, her voice barely audible. "I was watching your muscles move. It made me feel..."

"What?" I demanded, my thumb pressing against her lower lip, dragging it down. "What did it make you feel?"

"Safe," she whispered.

The word hit me like a slapshot to the chest.

Safe.

She looked at the violence of my body, the destructive potential stored in my muscles, and she didn't feel threatened. She felt secure. She saw a fortress.

My heart hammered against my ribs, a slow, heavy rhythm of possession.

You stay in the jar, I thought viciously. *You stay on the shelf where nothing can touch you.*

"Rook," I said, never taking my eyes off her.

"Yeah, Cap?"

"Open the gate."

"With pleasure."

Rook unlatched the gate. It swung open with a metallic groan.

There was no ice between us now. Just the rubber mat and the step up.

"Come here," I told her.

Mina stepped forward. She looked at the ice, then at me. "I don't have skates."

"You don't need them," I said.

I reached down. I grabbed her by the waist. My hands spanned her entirely, thumbs nearly touching at her navel. She gasped as I lifted her.

She was light. Terrifyingly light. A feather.

I pulled her over the threshold and onto the ice. But I didn't set her down. I couldn't. Her feet would slip. She would fall.

I held her against me, her feet dangling a foot off the ice. Her chest pressed against the hard plastic of my shoulder pads. Her hands flew up to grip my neck, her fingers tangling in my wet hair.

"Wrap your legs around me," I commanded.

She obeyed instantly. Her legs hooked around my waist. The friction of her thighs against my hips was exquisite torture.

"Got her?" Rook asked, skating in close behind me.

"I've got her."

Rook reached out and placed a hand on the small of her back, sandwiching her between us.

"She's cold again," Rook noted, sounding offended by the ambient temperature. "We need to stimulate blood flow."

Mina buried her face in the crook of my neck. She inhaled deeply, breathing in the sweat and the aggression.

"You smell like..." she trailed off.

"Like what?" I asked, turning my head so my lips brushed her ear.

"Like a storm," she murmured.

I tightened my grip on her thighs.

"We're done with practice," I announced. "We're going to the showers. You're coming with us."

"To watch?" she asked, pulling back slightly to look at me. Her gray eyes were wide, dilated, swimming with that same biological need that was currently rewiring my brain.

I looked at Rook. He was grinning, a wolfish, hungry expression that promised trouble.

"No," I said. "Not to watch."

I skated toward the exit tunnel, carrying her effortlessly, my precious, fragile burden.

"To participate."

Chapter Seven

TESTING THE THEORY

POV: Mercer

The rubber matting of the tunnel absorbed the bite of my skates, a dull, thumping rhythm that matched the hammering of my own pulse. I didn't put her down. I couldn't. The logic center of my brain, usually a fortress of cold calculation, had been breached by a primal need to keep her elevated, separated from the filth of the floor, pressed against the hard plastic of my chest protector.

Mina didn't struggle. Her arms remained looped around my neck, her face buried in the crook of my shoulder. She breathed in the reek of my exertion—sweat, ice shavings, and the sharp tang of adrenaline—as if it were oxygen.

Rook flank-skated me, his shoulder brushing mine, a wall of heat and agitation. He was vibrating. I could feel the energy radiating off him, a chaotic frequency that usually required a fistfight to settle. But tonight, his eyes weren't scanning for a threat. They were fixed on the curve of Mina's spine where her yellow cardigan had ridden up.

"She's too quiet," Rook growled, his voice echoing off the concrete walls of the tunnel. "Is she breathing?"

"I'm breathing," Mina mumbled against my neck. Her voice was small, a vibration against my collarbone.

"Good," Rook said. "Keep doing that. Don't stop."

We reached the locker room doors. I kicked them open. The heavy wood swung wide, revealing the sanctuary. This was our space. The air here was different—thick with the scent of tape, leather, and the unique, musk-heavy atmosphere of men who spent their lives colliding with one another. It was a place of violence and recovery, strictly off-limits to civilians. Especially female ones.

I walked to the center of the room, past the rows of empty stalls, to the oversized bench situated between Rook's locker and mine.

"Down," I murmured.

I lowered her. Her sneakers hit the floor, but I kept my hands on her waist for a second longer than necessary, steadying her. Or maybe steadying myself.

She looked absurd here. In the harsh fluorescent lighting, surrounded by black equipment bags and grey steel, her yellow sweater was a scream of color. She was a canary dropped into a coal mine.

"Sit," Rook ordered, pointing a gloved finger at the bench.

Mina sat. She pulled her knees together, clutching her bag in her lap. Her eyes darted around the room, taking in the discarded tape balls, the whiteboards covered in aggressive tactical scrawl, and finally, us.

We were monsters to her. I saw it in the way her pupils dilated. We were armored giants, smelling of aggression, towering over her with intent that was anything but professional.

"Lock the door, Rook," I said.

The lock clicked. The sound was final. The world outside—the press, the fans, the rules of biology—ceased to exist.

Rook didn't wait. He ripped his gloves off, throwing them into his stall with a wet *thud*. His helmet followed, clattering against the back wall. He ran a hand through his damp curls, his chest heaving.

"The air is better now," Rook said, inhaling deeply. He turned on Mina. "You changed the air."

"I... I just walked in," she whispered.

"No," I corrected. I started undoing the straps of my own gear. "You didn't just walk in. You saturated the environment."

I pulled off my gloves and placed them deliberately on the shelf. My hands felt strange—bare, hot, and empty. They twitched with the urge to grab something soft.

"Watch us," I commanded.

Mina nodded. Her gaze fixed on me as I reached for the laces of my jersey.

This wasn't a striptease. This was an unveiling of weaponry. We peeled the armor away to reveal the dense, scarred machinery underneath. I pulled the jersey over my head, tossing it aside. Then the shoulder pads. The Velcro tore with a ripping sound that seemed too loud in the quiet room.

When the heavy plastic shell hit the floor, I felt the cool air hit my sweat-slicked skin. I stood there in my compression shirt, the fabric adhering to every ridge of muscle in my torso.

Rook was less precise. He was tearing at his equipment, a frenzy of motion. He stripped to his waist, his chest bare, glistening with sweat. A map of violence was written on his skin—a fading bruise on his ribs from last week's game, a thick white scar across his pectoral from a skate blade three years ago.

He walked over to Mina. He didn't respect the bubble of personal space. He shattered it.

He planted his hands on the bench on either side of her hips, leaning down until they were nose to nose.

"You like seeing the damage?" Rook asked. His voice was a low rasp.

Mina didn't retreat. She leaned forward, her eyes tracing the scar on his chest. "Does it hurt?"

"Only when I breathe," Rook said, a dark amusement curling his lip. "Touch it."

Mina hesitated. Her hand trembled as she reached out. Her fingers were so small, pale and delicate against his tanned skin. She brushed her fingertips over the scar tissue.

Rook hissed. His head fell back, his eyes rolling shut.

"Fuck," he breathed. "Merc. Look at that."

I was looking. I was watching the way her touch seemed to short-circuit his nervous system. Rook, who needed impact to feel anything, was coming undone from the feather-light stroke of a biology student.

Jealousy, sharp and acidic, flooded my gut.

"That's enough," I snapped.

Rook's eyes snapped open. He growled, a low warning sound, but he pulled back. He knew the hierarchy.

"My turn," I said.

I stepped closer. I didn't lean down. I stood at my full height, forcing her to crane her neck to look at me. I unbuckled my pants, the heavy canvas falling to the floor. I stepped out of them, then the shin pads, peeling away the layers until I was standing in just my compression shorts.

I was exposed. Every inch of me was hard, functional muscle, built for checking and endurance. There was nothing soft about me.

"Stand up, Mina," I said.

She stood. The top of her head barely cleared my solar plexus. The size difference was a physical joyousness, a stark confirmation of the roles nature had assigned us.

"The sweater," I said. "Take it off."

Her eyes widened. "It's cold."

"We're hot," I countered. "We generate enough heat to keep you alive. Take it off. I want to see the variable."

Her hands went to the buttons. Her fingers fumbled. She was clumsy, nervous. It was endearing in a way that made my teeth ache.

When the yellow wool fell to the floor, she stood in a simple white t-shirt and leggings. She looked normal. Boring, even. And yet, the scent rolling off her—that maddening mix of sugar and rain—intensified.

I reached out. My hand engulfed her shoulder. I ran my palm down her arm, feeling the warmth of her skin through the thin cotton.

"Soft," I diagnosed. The data point hit me harder than a puck. "Rook, verify."

Rook was there instantly. He came up behind her. We boxed her in. A wall of muscle in front, a wall of muscle behind.

Rook wrapped his arms around her waist, pulling her back against his chest. He buried his face in her hair, inhaling loudly.

"Soft," Rook agreed, his voice muffled against her neck. "And small. I can feel her heart beating against my forearm. It's going so fast, Cap."

"She's afraid," I said, watching her face. Her lips were parted, her breath coming in shallow gasps.

"Are you afraid, Mina?" I asked. I slid my hand from her arm to her throat. I didn't squeeze. I just held her there, my thumb resting over her pulse.

"No," she whispered. Then, a correction. "Yes. But... not of you hurting me."

"What then?"

"Of you stopping," she confessed.

The words hung in the air, heavy and wet.

Rook groaned. He tightened his grip, lifting her slightly so she was on her toes, pressed fully against him. "She gets it. She understands the assignment."

"It's not an assignment," I murmured, stepping closer until my chest brushed the front of her shirt. "It's a requirement."

I leaned down. I needed to taste the air right next to her skin. I brushed my nose along the shell of her ear, inhaling the scent behind it.

She smelled clean. Innocent. It was a stark contrast to the locker room funk, a single note of purity in a symphony of grime.

"We need to wash," I said against her skin. "We're filthy."

"And she's too clean," Rook added. "She smells like soap and books. It's wrong. She should smell like us."

"Transfer," I stated.

"The showers?" Rook asked, a hopeful, predatory lilt in his voice.

"The showers."

Mina stiffened in Rook's arms. "I... I can't go in there. I'm dressed."

"Clothes are permeable," I informed her. "Water passes through them. It's basic physics, Mina."

I backed away, extending a hand. "Come."

Rook released her, but he grabbed her hand immediately, lacing his thick fingers through hers. I took the other one.

We led her to the shower block.

It was a large, tiled room with open heads along the walls. I reached in and twisted the heavy chrome handle. The pipes groaned, and then hot water blasted out, steam rising instantly to cloud the mirrors.

I stepped under the spray. The hot water hit my shoulders, sluicing away the sweat, loosening the tension in my neck. Rook stepped under the adjacent head.

Mina stood on the dry tiles, watching us. She looked at the water running down my chest, gathering in the waistband of my shorts. She looked at Rook, who had thrown his head back, letting the water soak his hair.

Her gaze was tactile. I could feel it sliding over my skin.

"In," I ordered.

She hesitated. "My shoes..."

"Leave them," Rook said.

She kicked off her sneakers. She stepped onto the wet tiles in her socks. It was a sensory nightmare for anyone else—wet socks on cold tile—but she didn't seem to notice. Her attention was consumed by the two giants bathing in front of her.

She stepped into the spray of my shower.

The water hit her instantly. Her white t-shirt absorbed the liquid, turning translucent, clinging to her skin like a second layer of dermis. Beneath it, the lace of her bra became visible, a pale outline against pale skin.

I stopped washing. My hands dropped to my sides.

She stood there, shivering slightly as the hot water soaked her hair, plastering the blonde strands to her skull. She looked like the drowned rat from the alley again.

And I had never wanted anything more in my life.

"Closer," I rasped.

She stepped into my personal space. The water beat down on both of us now. I reached out and put my hands on her waist. Her skin was warm under the wet cotton.

Rook abandoned his shower. He moved into ours. The stall was built for one large man, not two giants and a woman, but we made it work. We crowded her.

Rook dropped to his knees on the wet tile.

The water cascaded over his back. He wrapped his arms around her thighs, pressing his face into her stomach.

"Sugar and steam," Rook mumbled against her wet shirt. "Best smell in the world."

I looked down at him. He was worshipping her. The enforcer, the man who put people through glass for a living, was kneeling on hard tile just to be closer to her center.

And I wasn't disgusted. I was envious.

I ran my hands up her sides, feeling the curve of her ribs. She was so fragile. If I squeezed, she would break. That knowledge—her fragility—acted as a governor on my strength. It forced me to be precise.

"Look at us, Mina," I commanded softly.

She looked up. Water dripped from her eyelashes. Her lips were red, swollen from the heat.

"What do you see?" I asked.

"Everything," she choked out.

"Do you see the problem?" I moved one hand down, guiding hers to the waistband of my compression shorts.

She touched me. Her palm flat against the rigid length beneath the fabric.

I stopped breathing. Her hand was small, the heat of it searing through the wet spandex.

"We don't work like this," I told her, my voice tight. "We don't react to women. We never have. It's a closed circuit. Just him and me."

Rook hummed in agreement against her stomach, his hands kneading the backs of her thighs.

"But you..." I gritted my teeth as she squeezed, an experimental pressure that nearly sent me to my knees. "You hot-wire the system."

"Does it... does it feel bad?" she asked, her eyes wide with concern.

"It feels like dying," I lied. "It feels like starving and being handed a feast you don't know how to eat."

Rook stood up. Water streamed down his face. He looked manic.

"We can figure out how to eat," Rook said. He reached for the hem of her wet t-shirt. "We just need access."

"Not yet," I stopped him. My hand clamped over his wrist.

Rook snarled. "Why? She's right here. She's wet. She's ours."

"Because this is an experiment," I said, though my control was fraying like a worn rope. "And we need to establish the baseline before we introduce new variables."

I looked at Mina. She was trembling, not from cold, but from adrenaline.

"Turn around," I told her.

She turned. Her back was to me. I pulled her flush against my chest. I could feel every curve of her through our wet clothes.

Rook moved behind me. He wrapped his arms around my waist, his chin resting on my shoulder, looking down at her. We were a chain. A hierarchy.

"We're going to clean you," I whispered into her wet hair. "We're going to wash the world off you until you only smell like us. And then..."

"Then?" she asked breathlessly.

"Then we're going to see what you taste like fresh," Rook finished, biting the air near her neck.

I reached for the soap.

The bar was rough, industrial, meant for scrubbing grease and blood. It wasn't meant for her skin. I lathered it between my hands until it was just white foam.

Then I touched her.

I started at her neck, my large hands sliding over the wet skin, covering her completely. I washed her shoulders, my thumbs digging into the tension there. I washed her arms, encompassing her biceps with a single ring of fingers.

Rook grew impatient. He reached around me. His hands joined mine on her body.

Four hands. Massive, scarred, and demanding. We mapped her. We claimed her. We turned the shower into a ritual of ownership.

She tipped her head back against my chest and moaned.

The sound broke something in the room. It shattered the last pretense of scientific inquiry.

"Okay," I whispered, dropping the soap. "Hypothesis confirmed."

"Which one?" Rook asked, his hands sliding dangerously low on her stomach.

"That we can't let her go," I said. "She stays in the rotation."

Rook laughed, a dark, victorious sound against my ear. "She stays in the shower, Cap. We're not done."

"No," I agreed, my hands sliding under her wet shirt to find the warm, bare skin of her waist. "We're just getting started."

Chapter Eight

SUNLIGHT ON A ROUGH TONGUE

POV: Mercer

I shut off the water.

The silence that followed was heavy, broken only by the drip of water from the showerhead and the ragged sound of three people breathing in a space meant for one.

Mina shivered.

It wasn't the cold. The air in the locker room was stagnant and humid. She shivered because the atmosphere had shifted from hygiene to hunt. Her T-shirt clung to her skin, transparent and useless, plastering the curve of her small breasts against her ribs.

My hands were still on her waist. My thumbs dug into the soft flesh above her hips, verifying the lack of muscle tone. No abs. No oblique ridges. Just yield.

It was maddening.

"Table," I ordered.

I didn't wait for her to walk. I scooped her up. Her wet thighs slapped against my forearms, cold skin meeting hot muscle. She weighed nothing. I carried two hundred pounds of gear in my bag every day; she was a rounding error in my workout.

Rook followed, his footsteps heavy and wet on the rubber mats. He was prowling, his eyes fixed on the sway of her legs as they dangled from my hold.

I marched her to the trainer's table in the center of the room. It was black vinyl, smelling of antiseptic and tape adhesive. I set her down on the edge.

"Lie back," I said.

Mina hesitated. Her grey eyes darted between us, wide and terrified. "Mercer, I..."

"Lie back."

She obeyed. She lay flat, her wet hair fanning out like a dark halo on the black vinyl. Her sneakers dangled off the end of the table. She looked like a sacrifice. A clinical specimen prepared for dissection.

I stood between her knees.

For ten years, my world had been defined by hard angles. By the scrape of stubble against stubble, the bruise of hip bones clashing, the aggressive friction of a man's body against mine. I knew the geography of a male body like I knew the play of the puck. It made sense. Physics. Leverage. Force.

This? This made no sense.

She was soft curves and hidden valleys. There was no aggression here, only an invitation so potent it made my teeth ache.

"Take the leggings off," I told her.

Her hands shook as she reached for the waistband. The wet fabric fought her, clinging to her skin.

"Too slow," Rook growled from behind me.

I swatted his hand away before he could tear the fabric. "Patience. Let her do it. I want to see how she moves."

She peeled the leggings down. Inch by agonizing inch. Pale skin emerged, glowing under the harsh fluorescent lights. Knees. Thighs.

And then, the center of the problem.

She wasn't wearing underwear. The lace scraps must have stayed in her bag. She was bare.

I stopped breathing.

My brain tried to categorize the visual data, but the file was corrupted. There was nothing aggressive about it. It was a soft, pale vulnerability. Blonde curls, lighter than the ones on her head, guarded a secret I had spent my entire adult life ignoring.

"Fuck," Rook breathed. He leaned over my shoulder, his chest pressing into my back. "Cap. Look at that."

"I'm looking," I rasped.

"It's so... pretty." Rook sounded confused. "I thought it would be weird. Why isn't it weird?"

It *was* weird. It was terrifying. It was a biological weapon aimed straight at the fortress of my sexuality.

"Spread your legs," I said. My voice sounded like gravel grinding in a mixer.

Mina whimpered. "Mercer, please. You don't... you don't do this."

"I am doing this," I corrected. "I need to know."

"Know what?"

"If the taste matches the smell."

I gripped her ankles. My fingers wrapped completely around the delicate bones. I pushed her legs apart, locking her knees open.

The scent hit me.

It wasn't the locker room funk. It wasn't the metallic tang of blood or the sharpness of testosterone. It was concentrated sweetness. Rainwater and heated sugar. It rolled off her in waves, drowning out the smell of the floor cleaner, drowning out the smell of Rook, drowning out my own sanity.

I dropped to my knees.

The floor was hard against my shins. I didn't care. I settled between her open thighs, my hands sliding up to grip the backs of her knees, anchoring her.

At eye level, the view was devastating.

"Don't look," she gasped, trying to clamp her legs shut.

I held her firm. "I'm going to look. I'm going to map every inch of you."

I leaned in. The heat radiating from her was immense. My nose brushed the inside of her thigh, the skin impossibly soft against the roughness of my afternoon shadow.

I inhaled.

A jolt of electricity arced down my spine, settling heavily in my groin. My cock throbbed, a painful, insistent hammer against the zipper of my wet shorts.

"Open for me," I commanded softly against her skin.

I used my thumbs to part her.

Pink. glistening. Perfect.

The cognitive dissonance shattered. I didn't care that she was a woman. I didn't care that this violated every label the press had slapped on me for three years. I only cared that this specific, beautiful thing belonged to us.

I brought my mouth to her.

I didn't kiss her. I *claimed* her.

I licked—a long, broad stripe from bottom to top.

Mina screamed. It wasn't a word; it was a high, thin sound of pure shock. Her hips bucked off the table.

I clamped my hands tighter on her thighs, pinning her down.

"Still," I growled against her. "Take it."

I went back in. The taste was a revelation. Sweet, salty, intoxicating. It was like drinking cool water after running a marathon in the desert. I had expected it to be foreign. I expected to hate the texture. Instead, it felt like coming home to a house I didn't know I owned.

I wasn't gentle. I didn't know how to be gentle with my mouth. I used my tongue like a weapon, probing, swirling, demanding a response.

She tasted of arousal and surrender.

"Mercer!" She sobbed my name, her hands flying down to tangle in my wet hair. She tried to pull me off. Or maybe push me closer.

"Let me help," Rook said.

He moved to the head of the table. He didn't touch her face. He grabbed her wrists, pinning her arms above her head. He leaned down, his face inches from hers upside down.

"Watch him," Rook ordered her. "Look at what the Captain is doing for you. He's on his knees, Mina. For you."

I groaned, the vibration buzzing against her sensitive flesh.

I found the small, hard pearl at the top. The trigger.

I focused on it with the same obsessive intensity I applied to game tape. Isolation. Pressure. Speed.

I swirled my tongue around it, teasing the edges before flattening the muscle and flicking hard.

Mina's back arched off the table. Her heels dug into my shoulders.

"Please," she begged. "Too much. It's too much."

"Not enough," I mumbled against her. "Not nearly enough."

I increased the pace. I sucked, drawing the swollen flesh into my mouth, treating her like a piece of fruit I intended to bruise. My stubble scraped her inner thighs, leaving red marks on the porcelain skin. Good. I wanted to leave a mark. I wanted her to look at herself in the mirror tomorrow and see the ghost of my mouth on her body.

She started to unravel.

Her breathing turned into fractured gasps. Her scent spiked, turning heavier, muskier. The smell of a female in heat.

It drove me feral.

The civilized part of my brain—the Captain, the strategist—went dark. The animal took the controls.

I grabbed her hips, lifting her basin to meet my mouth. I devoured her. I ate her like a starving man, my tongue working in a relentless, punishing rhythm. Slurp. Lick. Suck.

"Rook," she cried out. "Rook, help me!"

"Take it," Rook whispered, his voice dark with envy. He held her wrists tighter. "Break for him, Mina. Show us what you look like when you fall apart."

She fell.

Her body went rigid. A convulsing tremor started in her core and radiated outward. Her inner muscles clamped down on my tongue, pulsing, squeezing.

I didn't stop. I kept going, drinking every drop of her release, forcing her to ride out the aftershocks until she was sobbing, boneless and wrecked.

Only then did I pull back.

My face was wet. My chin dripped with her.

I stayed on my knees for a moment, waiting for the room to stop spinning. The silence returned, but it wasn't empty now. It was filled with the sound of her jagged breathing.

Slowly, I stood up.

My knees cracked. I wiped my mouth with the back of my hand, but I didn't wipe it off. I licked the stripe of moisture from my knuckles.

I looked at her.

She was destroyed. Her chest heaved. Her legs were still splayed open, trembling uncontrollably. Her eyes were glazed, unfocused, staring up at the ceiling tiles as if trying to reassemble her reality.

Rook released her wrists. He looked at me. His eyes were black holes. He looked at my mouth, then at her center, then back at me.

"Well?" Rook asked. His voice was tight, strained.

I walked to the head of the table. I leaned down until my lips brushed her ear.

"Sweet," I confirmed, my voice rough with a hunger that hadn't been sated, only awakened. "She tastes like mine."

Mina turned her head. Her eyes found mine. There was no fear left in them. Only a terrifying, absolute adoration.

"Again," she whispered.

I smiled. It was a sharp, dangerous thing.

"We have all night, little mouse. And Rook hasn't even had a turn."

Chapter Nine

THE SOLE DEVIATION

POV: Mina

The ceiling tiles were counting down to her destruction. One, two, three cracks in the plaster above the trainer's table.

Then she lost the ability to count.

The world narrowed down to the wet, devastating heat between her thighs. Mercer wasn't kissing her. Kissing implied affection, romance, a softness that didn't exist in this cold, steel-lined room. He was devouring her. He was taking her apart with the same terrifying, methodical precision he used to dismantle opposing defensive lines on the ice.

Her heels dug into the black vinyl. Friction burned against her skin, but it was distant, a dull roar compared to the sharp, electric current snapping through her nervous system.

"Don't close your legs," Mercer ordered against her sensitive flesh. The vibration of his voice traveled straight through her pelvis, rattling her teeth.

Mina whimpered. She tried to obey. Logic told her to push him away, to zip her jeans, to run back to the safety of her dorm where the air didn't smell like musk and predatory intent. But her body was a traitor. Her hips lifted off the table, seeking more pressure, not less.

Mercer didn't hesitate. He adjusted his grip on her thighs, his fingers bruising-tight, anchoring her in place. He treated her body like a puzzle he had already solved. He knew exactly where the nerve endings clustered, exactly how much suction made her breath hitch, and exactly when to switch from long, languid strokes to a punishing, rhythmic flicker.

He was ruining her.

Rook stood at the head of the table. He wasn't touching her, not really. His hands hovered over her shoulders, creating a cage of air and heat. She looked up, desperate for an anchor in the storm, and found him watching the junction of her legs with a focus that bordered on religious mania.

"Look at the color," Rook whispered, his voice wrecked. "She's so pink. And he's... fuck, look at his jaw working."

Mina squeezed her eyes shut. The shame should have been crushing. She was a biology student, a nobody, splayed open for the two most famous, exclusively gay men in the city. But the shame burned up in the atmosphere of their obsession.

Mercer accelerated.

He flattened his tongue against the swollen pearl of her clitoris and hummed. The sensation was blinding. A white-hot spike drove through her belly.

"Mercer," she gasped. The air left her lungs in a jagged rush. "I can't... I'm going to..."

"Do it," Mercer growled. He sucked harder.

The tension coiled tight in her lower belly, a spring wound to the breaking point. She clawed at the vinyl sheets. She needed something to hold, something to ground her before she flew apart.

Rook's hand slammed down next to her head.

Mina grabbed it blindly. Her small fingers wrapped around his thick wrist, her nails digging into the tendons. He didn't flinch. He leaned in, his dark curls brushing her forehead, his breathing syncing with hers—ragged, desperate.

"Let go, mouse," Rook urged. "Break."

And she did.

The orgasm hit her like a physical blow. Her entire body bowed upward. A scream tore from her throat, echoing off the metal lockers. Muscle spasms rocked through her, wave after paralyzing wave of pleasure that wiped her mind clean of everything but the feeling of Mercer's mouth drinking her down.

He didn't stop. He chased the aftershocks, milking every last drop of reaction from her trembling limbs until she lay boneless, gasping, staring up at those three cracks in the ceiling through a haze of tears.

Silence crashed back into the room.

It was heavy, thick with the scent of sex and the hum of the ventilation system. Keep breathing. In. Out. Her heart hammered a frantic rhythm against her ribs, refusing to slow down.

Mercer pulled back.

He stayed on his knees for a beat, head bowed, shoulders heaving. Then he stood.

Mina watched him, unable to look away.

He was terrifying.

He stood six-foot-six in his compression shorts, a monolith of pale, scarred muscle. His chest was a wall of hard ridges and valleys, the pectorals defined and immobile as stone. But it was his face that stole the air from her lungs. His lips were wet, swollen, and red with the evidence of what he'd just done. A single drop of moisture clung to his chin.

He wiped it away with the back of his hand, his blue eyes cold, analytical, assessing the damage.

He looked like a god who had just descended to taste a mortal offering and found it acceptable.

Then her gaze drifted to his hands. They hung at his sides, twitching slightly. Those hands. They were monstrosities of function—broad palms, thick, square fingers calloused from gripping a stick, knuckles scarred from fighting. They were twice the size of hers. He could crush her skull with a casual squeeze, yet those same massive, devastating instruments had just held her open with a steadiness that made her want to weep.

"Hydration," Mercer said. His voice was a rasp, stripped of its usual smooth command.

He turned and walked to the cooler in the corner. His back was a V-shape of daunting width, the muscles shifting under his skin like coiled snakes.

Rook didn't move. He was still leaning over her, his pupils blown so wide his eyes looked black.

"You smell like him now," Rook noted. He sounded jealous. He reached out and touched her wet cheek. "And you taste like... victory."

Mina sat up. The movement was clumsy; her limbs felt like jelly. She pulled her knees to her chest, trying to reclaim some scrap of modesty, though it was laughably late for that.

Mercer returned. He held out a paper cup of water.

"Drink."

Mina took it. Her hand shook so hard the water sloshed over the rim. Mercer's hand shot out, steadying the cup, guiding it to her lips. His fingers brushed hers. The contact sent a fresh jolt of electricity through her, hot and unwelcome.

She drank. The cold water shocked her system back online.

"This..." Her voice cracked. She cleared her throat. "This doesn't make sense."

"Biology is rarely sensible," Mercer said. He leaned against a locker bank, crossing his massive arms over his chest. "It's messy. It reacts to stimuli."

"You're gay," Mina whispered. The words hung in the air, an accusation and a fact. "You... both of you. Everyone knows. You don't like women."

"We don't," Rook agreed heavily. He moved to stand next to Mercer.

The visual impact of them side-by-side was overwhelming. Fire and Ice. Chaos and Control. They took up all the space, sucking the oxygen out of the room. Rook was broader, thicker through the shoulders, a brawler built for impact. Mercer was taller, leaner but denser, built for leverage. They were masterpieces of male aggression.

And they were looking at her like she was the only water source in a desert.

"We don't want women," Mercer corrected, his tone clinical, as if explaining a complex defensive play on the whiteboard. "I have never looked at a female and felt a spike in heart rate. Never felt the urge to pursue. The anatomy... it doesn't appeal."

He gestured vaguely toward her.

"Until you."

Mina pulled her oversized t-shirt down over her knees. "Why? Because I'm small? Because I'm easy to push around?"

"Because you're quiet," Rook said. He paced a tight circle, agitated. "Other women are loud. They smell like perfume and ambition. You smell like..." He inhaled deeply, his nostrils flaring. "Peace. And sugar. It hot-wires the brain."

"It's a glitch," Mercer stated. He pushed off the locker and took a step toward the table. "A physiological anomaly. We are under immense pressure. Cortisol levels remain critically high during the season. We require an outlet."

"An outlet," Mina repeated. The word tasted bitter. "Like a punching bag?"

"No," Mercer said sharply. "We have punching bags. We hit them until they break. We don't want to break you."

He stopped in front of her. He placed his hands on the edge of the table, caging her legs.

"We want to keep you," he said. "The way a dragon keeps gold. Useless, perhaps, for survival. But necessary for the hoard."

"I'm not a stress toy," Mina argued, though the fight was weak in her voice. "I'm a student. I have a life. I have exams."

"We'll help you study," Rook offered immediately. "We have money. We can buy you tutors. The best ones."

"I don't need money," Mina snapped. She looked up at Mercer. "What do you need?"

Mercer held her gaze. The blue of his irises seemed to freeze her in place.

"We need to touch you," he said simply. "We need to be near you. When you aren't in the room, the noise comes back. The aggression turns inward. We start tearing each other apart."

He reached out and tucked a stray strand of blonde hair behind her ear. His knuckles grazed her jaw.

"You are the buffer," he whispered. "The soft place for the rage to land."

Mina's heart thudded against her ribs. It was insane. It was toxic. It was the most dangerous proposition she had ever heard. Two apex predators asking to use her as a pacifier.

And yet.

She looked at the dark circles under Rook's eyes. She looked at the tension vibrating in Mercer's jaw. She felt the way the room seemed to center around her, a gravity well of protection.

She had spent three years at this university feeling invisible. Too small. Too quiet. Too nerdy for the athletes, too distracted for the academics. She walked through halls like a ghost.

Here, under the harsh fluorescent lights, with her scent on Mercer's mouth, she was the most important thing in the universe.

"Just... physical?" she asked. Her voice was barely a whisper.

"Just friction," Mercer lied. She knew it was a lie. He knew it was a lie. But it was a necessary structure to hang their madness on. "You come to us. We take care of the stress. You leave. No feelings. No complications. We remain who we are. You remain who you are."

"A medical necessity," Rook added, grinning. It was a sharp, wolfish expression. "Like a prescription."

Mina looked at Rook's forearms, the veins distinct ropes under the tanned skin. She looked at the bulge in Mercer's shorts, terrifyingly evident.

Her body hummed. A second wave of heat pooled low in her belly, shocking her. She shouldn't want this. She should be running.

But God, she wanted to see what the Enforcer would do if she said yes.

"Okay," she whispered.

The air in the room shifted instantly. The tension didn't vanish; it changed flavor. From uncertainty to possession.

Mercer exhaled, a long sound of relief. "Smart girl."

"Wait," Rook said. He stepped forward, crowding into the space. "The agreement starts now?"

"Yes," Mercer said.

"Good." Rook's eyes dropped to Mina's lips. "Because you had your turn, Cap. But I haven't tasted the glitch yet."

Mercer didn't push him away. He didn't snarl. He just stepped back, giving his partner space, his eyes darkening with a shared, voyeuristic hunger.

"Go ahead," Mercer permitted. "Check the data."

Mina watched Rook lean down, his shadow falling over her, blotting out the light. She realized with a sudden, dizzying clarity that she wasn't the scientist in this lab anymore.

She was the experiment.

And she didn't want the testing to stop.

Chapter Ten

Hard Instruction

POV: Mercer

Mercer stepped back, creating a vacuum of space beside the vinyl table where Mina lay wreaked and glowing.

The air in the locker room felt pressurized, heavy enough to crack ribs. My own lungs burned with the shallow, rapid rhythm of a man who had just run a suicide drill, but the exertion hadn't touched my muscles. It had hammered straight into the primitive stem of my brain.

I wiped the back of my hand across my mouth. The taste of her—salt, sweet, and something unmistakably *female*—lingered on my tongue. It was a sensory violation of everything I knew about myself. For twenty-eight years, my world had been hard angles, rough stubble, and the friction of bodies that mirrored my own. Women were background noise. Static.

She wasn't static. She was the signal.

"Your turn," I rasped, my voice sounding like gravel grinding in a mixer.

Rook didn't move immediately. He stood at the foot of the table, his massive chest heaving, his dark curls plastered to his forehead with sweat. He looked like a predator confused by a trap that didn't hurt. His gaze wasn't on me. It was fixed on the juncture of Mina's thighs, where the evidence of my hunger glistened on her pale skin.

"She's shaking," Rook whispered.

"She's overwhelmed," I corrected, though the tremor in Mina's legs sent a dark, possessive spike through my chest. "Adrenaline. Endorphins. It's a chemical cocktail."

"She looks broken." Rook's hands flexed at his sides, opening and closing in a rhythm of restrained violence. "Did you break her, Merc?"

"No." I moved to the head of the table, looking down at her. Mina's eyes were half-lidded, glazed with a stupor that I recognized. I'd seen it in Rook's eyes after a fight, after a win. Total surrender to the moment. "She's not broken. She's open."

Mina turned her head on the black vinyl. Her grey eyes found Rook. She didn't pull her legs closed. She didn't try to hide the damp, swollen reality of her body.

"Rook," she treathed. A soft, airy sound.

That single syllable snapped the last cable holding Rook's control.

He moved. He didn't walk; he stalked, closing the distance to the side of the table in a blur of motion. He crowded her, his thighs bumping against the edge of the table, looming over her small form like a thunderhead.

"I don't know how," Rook confessed, his voice tight with frustration. He looked at me, panic flaring in the black depths of his eyes. "I don't know how to touch this without ruining it. She's too soft, Cap. My hands... they're not made for this."

He held up his hands—wide, scarred, tape-residue sticky, instruments designed to break jaws and grip sticks.

"It's just flesh," I said.

The lie tasted like ash. It wasn't just flesh. It was a biological imperative wrapped in silk. It was a deity that demanded an offering I didn't know I had to give. But Rook needed the Captain right now. He needed the strategist, not the man who wanted to fall to his knees and worship the curve of a hip bone.

"It's resilient," I added, stepping closer to his back. "She can take you."

"Show me," Rook demanded.

He reached out and grabbed my wrist, dragging me into the space with him. He positioned me behind him, then shifted so we flanked her, creating a wall of heat and muscle that blocked out the rest of the room.

"Touch her," I ordered.

Rook hesitated. He lowered his hand toward her stomach. His fingers trembled. When his palm finally made contact with the soft skin of her belly, he flinched as if he'd touched a live wire.

"Fuck," he hissed. "She's hot. Burning."

"Follow the heat," I instructed.

Rook slid his hand lower. He watched his own fingers moving against her skin with a kind of horrified fascination. His hand was massive on her, spanning her entire lower abdomen. The contrast was a visual assault—his tanned, scarred skin against her creamy pallor, his brute strength hovering over her fragility.

Mina gasped when his fingers brushed the curls at the top of her thighs. Her hips bucked, a reflex.

Rook froze. "I'm hurting her."

"You aren't," Mina whispered. She reached down, her small hands grabbing his thick wrist. She didn't push him away. She pulled him down. "Please. Rook. I want to feel you."

I want to feel you.

The words hit me like a check into the boards. Jealousy, sharp and acidic, flared in my gut. I wanted to be the only one. I wanted to be the only thing she ever felt. But looking at Rook—my partner, my anchor, the only other person on this planet who understood the monstrous silence inside our heads—I realized I wanted him to have this too. I needed him to be just as infected as I was.

"Do it," I growled near his ear.

Rook groaned. He let her guide his hand.

He didn't have my clinical detachment. He didn't have the patience to map her anatomy. He went on instinct. He slid two fingers into her, deep and unhesitating.

Mina cried out—a sharp, high sound that echoed off the metal lockers.

"Too rough," I warned, my hand landing on Rook's shoulder, gripping the deltoid hard enough to bruise.

"No," Mina panted. Her head threw back, exposing the long, white line of her throat. "No, it's... it's full. He's so big."

Rook's head dropped. He stared at where his hand disappeared inside her. A shudder racked his massive frame.

"So tight," Rook choked out. "Merc, it's... it's gripping me. Like a fist."

"I know," I murmured.

"It feels..." Rook shook his head, sweat flying from his hair. "It feels like coming home."

He began to move. It wasn't the rhythmic, practiced stroke of a lover. It was the experimental, desperate thrust of a man discovering a new element. He twisted his wrist, his thick fingers stretching her, filling her.

Mina was unraveling again. Her hips lifted to meet him, her heels digging into the vinyl. She made small, wet noises that tore at my composure.

But Rook was drowning.

I could feel it in the tension radiating off him. He was lost in the sensation of her softness, terrified by the alien nature of it. He was drifting away from the anchor of who we were.

"Rook," I said sharply.

He didn't answer. He was panting, his eyes blown wide, lost in the sight of her flushed face.

He needed grounding. He needed the circuit to close.

I stepped in behind him, pressing my chest to his back. I wrapped an arm around his waist, locking him against me. I could feel his heart hammering against his ribs, beating in sync with mine.

"Look at me," I commanded.

Rook turned his head. His eyes were wild, frantic. "I can't stop. I can't stop touching her."

"Don't stop," I said. "But don't get lost."

I leaned in and crushed my mouth to his.

The kiss was violent. Familiar. It tasted of us—of mint gum, coffee, and the metallic tang of adrenaline. It was the taste of three years of partnership, of shared victories and shared beds. It was the grounding wire for the electricity arcing through the room.

Rook made a noise in his throat, a desperate, grateful growl. He kissed me back hard, his teeth clashing against mine, his tongue sweeping into my mouth to claim the space.

We devoured each other. We stood there, two giants tangled together, while his hand continued to work inside the girl on the table.

It shouldn't have worked. It should have been grotesque. But as I kissed him, as I felt the rough stubble of his jaw against mine and the solid wall of his muscle against my chest, the panic in my own chest subsided.

We weren't losing ourselves to a woman. We were bringing her in. We were absorbing her into the unit.

Mina sobbed.

The sound broke the kiss. We didn't pull apart, just pulled back an inch, breathing each other's air. We looked down at her.

She was watching us. Her eyes were wide, filled with tears, fixed on our joined mouths. She didn't look disgusted. She looked... awestruck.

"More," she whispered. "Don't stop kissing. Please."

"She likes it," Rook murmured against my lips. A dark, wicked amusement curled the corner of his mouth. "The little pervert likes watching us."

"She's ours," I confirmed. "She likes what we are."

Rook turned his attention back to her, but he kept one hand gripping the back of my neck, holding me there. He needed the contact. He needed to know I was watching him take her.

He increased the pace. His arm muscles bunched and released under my hand as he pumped into her. The sound of wet friction filled the quiet room—a lewd, slapping rhythm that should have been shameful but sounded like victory.

"Use your thumb," I instructed, watching the way Mina's body tightened. "She likes the pressure. High up."

Rook obeyed. He ground the pad of his thumb against her clitoris while his fingers curved inside her, hitting a spot that made her toes curl.

"Here?" Rook asked, watching her face contort.

"There," I confirmed.

"Open your eyes, Mina," Rook growled. "Look at us. Look at who owns you."

Mina's eyes fluttered open. She looked at Rook, looming above her, sweat dripping from his nose. She looked at me, standing behind him like a shadow, my hand on his chest, claiming him while he claimed her.

"yours," she gasped.

The word was the trigger.

Rook slammed into her, his hand moving with a blurring speed. Mina screamed, her body arching off the table, caught in a seizure of pleasure so intense it looked painful. She clamped down on his fingers, milking him, her inner muscles pulsing in a rhythm that drove Rook to the edge of sanity.

"Fuck, fuck, *fuck*," Rook chanted, burying his face in the crook of my neck as he rode out her orgasm with his hand. He bit down on my trapezius muscle, a sharp pain that grounded me, kept me from tearing the room apart.

We held her through the aftershocks. We held her until the spasms stopped and she collapsed back onto the vinyl, limp and gasping, her skin flushed a deep, blotchy rose.

Rook slowly withdrew his hand. He stared at his fingers, slick and shining with her fluids.

He didn't wipe it off. He brought his hand to his face and inhaled, his eyes rolling back in his head.

"Sweet," he agreed with my earlier assessment. "Like sugar and rain."

He turned to me then, his expression raw, stripped of all defenses. "We can't give this back, Merc. We can't let her go back to the dorms. Not after this."

"No," I said. The decision had been made the moment she walked through the door. "We keep her."

Mina made a small, distressing sound. She tried to sit up, but her arms gave out. She slumped back, shivering violently. The adrenaline was crashing, and the cold air of the locker room was biting into her damp skin.

"She's freezing," Rook noted, his voice dropping into that low, rumbling register he used when he was worried.

"Floor," I said.

Establish dominance? No. Establish a nest.

I grabbed a stack of clean towels from the shelf—thick, white, industrial cotton. I threw them onto the rubber mats in the corner, away from the draft of the door, creating a makeshift bed. Then I grabbed our discarded jerseys.

Rook understood. He moved to the table. He didn't ask her to move. He scooped her up, cradling her against his bare chest like she was made of glass. Mina curled into him instantly, burying her face in his neck, seeking his heat.

He carried her to the corner and lowered her onto the towels.

She looked tiny there, a pale speck against the dark rubber floor. Rook sat down heavily beside her, leaning his back against the locker. He pulled her into his lap, ignoring the dampness of her clothes, ignoring the absurdity of the tableau.

I walked over and dropped the jerseys on top of them. My number 24. His number 88. Heavy, oversized fabric that smelled like us.

Rook adjusted them, tucking the heavy knit around her shoulders, covering her legs, cocooning her until only her face was visible. She blinked up at him, her eyelashes wet, her lips swollen and red.

She looked safe. She looked claimed.

I sat down on her other side, my shoulder pressing against Rook's. We boxed her in. A fortress of flesh and bone.

Rook ran a thumb over her cheek, wiping away a stray tear. The aggression had drained out of him, replaced by a terrifyingly focused calm.

"Better?" he asked her softly.

Mina nodded, her eyes drifting shut. She snuggled deeper into the pile of jerseys, breathing in the scent of the team, the scent of the men who had just used her to fix their own broken wiring.

"Warm," she mumbled.

Rook looked at me over her head. He smiled—a genuine, exhausted, boyish thing that I hadn't seen in months.

"Much better," he said.

Chapter Eleven

A Singular Hunger

POV: Mercer

The elevator ascent was silent, a vertical line drawn straight up into the darker sky above the city. The numbers on the digital display ticked upward—30, 31, 32—mimicking the rising pressure in my own skull.

Mina stood between us.

She didn't reach my shoulder. She barely cleared Rook's elbow. In the reflection of the brushed steel doors, the three of us looked like a physiological joke. Two monsters carved from granite and scar tissue, flanking a creature made of spun sugar and breakable bones.

She wore my hoodie. The hem hit her mid-thigh, swallowing her hands completely. It was a size XXL, draped over her petite frame like a tent. seeing my name across her back, seeing *my* number distorted by the curve of her small spine, did something terrible to my serotonin levels. It flooded the logic centers with a thick, possessive sludge.

Mine.

The thought was inaccurate. *Ours.*

Rook shifted his weight. The small space vibrated with his impatience. He wasn't looking at the numbers. He was staring at the back of her neck, where a loose tendril of blonde hair had escaped her messy bun. His pupils were blown so wide his eyes looked like black holes.

The doors slid open.

Our penthouse spanned the entire top floor. We bought it for the isolation, not the view. It was a fortress of glass, gray leather, and polished concrete. No warmth. No clutter. Just open space and silence.

Mina stepped out. Her sneakers squeaked on the marble floor.

She stopped. She looked at the sprawling living room, the floor-to-ceiling windows overlooking the city lights, the massive, sectional sofa that cost more than a rookie's contract.

"It's... cold," she whispered.

"It's temperature controlled," I corrected, stepping up behind her. "Sixty-eight degrees. Optimal for recovery."

"No," she said, wrapping her arms around herself, hugging my hoodie tighter. "I mean it feels cold. Like nobody lives here."

"We don't live here," Rook grunted, kicking the door shut behind us with his heel. "We wait here between games."

He walked past her, shedding his jacket in motion. He threw it onto a chair without looking. His focus remained locked on her. He was prowling. The enclosure was smaller now, the air thinner.

"Take it off," I said.

Mina spun around. Her gray eyes went wide. "Here? In the... living room?"

"Everywhere," I said. I walked to the kitchen island—a slab of black marble that looked like an altar. I learned against it, crossing my arms. "I need to see the variable in the environment. I need to see if you fit."

"I fit in the locker room," she argued weakly.

"That was neutral ground," I countered. "This is the hive. This is where we sleep. Where we bleed. Where we fuck."

Rook made a low noise in his throat at the word. He moved behind the sofa, gripping the leather backrest until the material creaked.

"Do it, mouse," Rook ordered. "The hoodie is too big. It hides the data."

Mina hesitated. Her fingers fumbled with the hem of the sweatshirt.

She pulled it up.

The motion was slow, agonizing. First her thighs appeared, pale and smooth against the dark gray of the room. Then the curve of her waist, an indentation so deep and soft it looked impossible. Then the swell of her ribs.

When her head popped through the neck hole, her hair was a static mess. She dropped the hoodie on the floor.

She stood in the center of our living room in a white t-shirt and nothing else.

It wasn't enough.

"The shirt," I said. My voice dropped an octave, scraping the bottom of my register. "All of it. Skin only."

She bit her lip. A flush rose on her chest, a map of heat spreading upward. She reached for the hem of the t-shirt.

When she lifted it, the air in the room seemed to vanish.

She was naked.

Against the stark, brutal minimalism of our apartment, she was a shock of biological perfection. Soft. curved. Pink where we were gray. Round where we were sharp.

Rook vaulted the couch.

He didn't stick the landing; he didn't care. He landed heavy and moved fast, closing the distance between them in two strides. He stopped inches from her, his chest heaving.

"Look at the size of her," Rook breathed. He sounded devastated. "Merc, look at her next to the coffee table. She's tiny."

I pushed off the island. I walked over.

The contrast was sickeningly sweet. My furniture was oversized, built to accommodate men who were six-foot-six and two hundred and forty pounds of dense muscle. Next to the heavy oak table, next to the sprawling leather sofa, next to *us*, she looked like a doll. A fragile, collector's item that had wandered out of its display case.

I circled her.

My eyes traced the line of her spine, the flare of her hips. I cataloged the lack of scars. The lack of bruises. The lack of definition.

"Turn around," I commanded.

She turned.

Her ass was a heart-shaped invitation. Soft. Yielding.

I reached out. My hand engulfed her shoulder. My fingers were long enough to touch her collarbone and her scapula at the same time. The heat of her skin scorched my palm.

"Fragile," I diagnosed.

"Breakable," Rook agreed. He reached out and wrapped his hand around her upper arm. His thumb and forefinger met easily. He could snap her humerus like a dry twig.

The realization didn't make me want to retreat. It made the monster inside my chest roar. It demanded I wrap myself around her, layer my concrete density over her softness until she was completely insulated from the world.

"Up," I told Rook. "Put her on the island."

Rook didn't ask questions. He bent down, scooped her up. One arm under her knees, one around her back. She gasped, clutching his shoulders.

He carried her to the black marble slab. He set her down.

The stone was cold. She hissed as her bare skin made contact, her thighs pressing against the dark, polished surface.

I stepped between her knees.

The view was catastrophic to my self-control. Her legs dangled, barely reaching my mid-thigh. Her center—that sweet, wet deviation that had ruined us in the locker room—was directly at eye level if I leaned forward just an inch.

"Spread them," I said.

She opened for me.

I placed my hands on the marble on either side of her hips, trapping her. I leaned in.

"Rook," I said, never taking my eyes off the pink flesh waiting for me. "Come here. Stand behind her."

Rook moved. He climbed onto the island behind her. He knelt on the marble, towering over her seated form. He wrapped his arms around her from behind, his hands covering her breasts.

His hands were too big. They swallowed her. His tanned skin against her pale curves looked violent. His chin rested on top of her head.

"She smells like sugar," Rook groaned into her hair. "Even here. Even with the city smell. She cuts right through it."

"She is the signal," I murmured.

I looked at the tableau. My partner—the man I had gone to war with for three seasons, the man whose body I knew as well as my own—holding this tiny, soft thing. We were gray and black and scarred. She was gold and cream and perfect.

We were a fortress. She was the treasure we kept in the vault.

"Touch her," I ordered Rook. "Show me the difference."

Rook's hands squeezed her breasts. He tweaked her nipples, his rough thumbs dragging over the sensitive peaks.

Mina cried out, her head falling back against Rook's chest.

"Soft," Rook marveled. "No muscle. Just... give. Merc, it's like touching a cloud."

I stepped closer. My groin brushed her knees.

"And you?" I asked her. "What do you feel?"

Mina opened her eyes. They were hazy, drugged with the proximity of two apex predators.

"Big," she whispered. "Hard. Everywhere."

"Good." I reached out and ran a finger down her sternum, between Rook's encircling arms. "You are surrounded by hard things. Stone. Steel. Us. You are the only soft thing in this zip code."

I let my hand drift lower. Past her navel. To the blonde curls.

"And this..." I brushed the back of my fingers against her slit. "This is the only wet thing."

She shuddered. Moisture coated my knuckle instantly.

"Leaking," I noted. "Inefficient."

"It's not inefficient," Rook growled, biting her shoulder gently. "It's lubrication. It's preparation."

"For what?" I asked, testing the logic.

"For the invasion," Rook said.

The word hung in the air. Invasion.

It wasn't a romantic term. It was a tactical one.

I looked at Rook. He was staring at me over her head. His expression was stark. He wasn't thinking about dinner or dates. He was thinking about filling the space inside her. He was thinking about claiming the one part of the world that didn't fight back.

"The bedroom," I decided.

"Bed," Rook agreed.

He didn't wait for her to move. He stood up, lifting her with him effortlessly. She dangled in his arms, her feet kicking the air.

I led the way.

The hallway was long and dark, lined with framed jerseys and trophies. Meaningless metal. The real prize was being carried behind me.

I kicked the double doors open.

Our bedroom was a cavern. Blackout curtains. A bed that was custom-built, seven feet by eight feet, a sprawling landscape of charcoal sheets.

Rook walked past me and tossed her onto the mattress.

She bounced. The mattress absorbed her weight without a sound. She scrambled backward, looking small and lost in the center of the vast grey expanse.

I walked to the edge of the bed. I started unbuckling my belt.

The sound of the leather snapping through the loops was loud in the quiet room.

"Watch," I told her.

Mina froze. Her eyes locked on my hands.

I pushed my trousers down. I stepped out of them. I pulled the compression shirt over my head.

Normally, stripping was mundane. A transition from work to rest. Now, it felt like arming a weapon. I revealed the machinery. The dense pectorals, the ridges of my abdominals, the thick scars on my hips from board battles.

I stood there in my briefs.

Then I took those off too.

Mina's breath hitched. Her gaze dropped.

I was hard. painfully, aggressively hard. My cock was heavy, thick with blood, twitching with a heartbeat of its own. It was a weapon of war, not an instrument of love.

"Too big," she whispered. The fear in her voice was genuine. "Mercer... it won't fit."

"It fits," I said. "Biology adapts."

Rook was stripping beside me. He was faster, tearing his clothes off until he stood naked. He was broader than me, thicker. His cock was a dense, dark distinct shape, angry and insistent.

We stood side by side at the foot of the bed. Two giants.

The visual data confirmed her hypothesis. We were too big. She was five feet of nothing. We were over thirteen feet of combined male aggression.

"We're going to split her," Rook said. He didn't sound worried. He sounded eager.

"We're going to stretch her," I corrected. "We're going to rewire her until she can take it."

I climbed onto the bed. The mattress dipped under my weight. I crawled toward her on hands and knees. A predator closing in on a trapped animal.

Mina scrambled back until she hit the headboard. Nowhere left to go.

I loomed over her. I planted my hands on the pillow on either side of her head. I lowered my body until I was hovering inches above her.

My chest completely eclipsed her vision. My shoulders blocked out the ceiling.

"Do you know why we brought you here?" I asked.

"To... to use me?" she squeaked.

"To calibrate," I said. "We need to know if you break."

Rook crawled up behind me. He didn't wait his turn. He moved to the side, gripping her ankle. he dragged her leg out, pinning it to the mattress.

"She won't break," Rook said. "She's elastic. Look at her skin."

He ran a hand up her inner thigh. His palm covered the entire distance from knee to hip.

"Soft," I repeated, the word becoming a prayer.

I lowered my hips. My cock brushed her stomach. A hot, heavy brand.

She flinched.

"Don't move," I ordered.

I slid down. I positioned myself. The head of my cock rested against her entrance.

It was absurd. The scale was wrong. It looked like trying to park a tank in a bicycle shed.

"Rook," I said. "Prepare the site."

Rook understood. He reached between us. His fingers—slick with saliva he'd just applied—found her opening. He pushed inside. One finger. Two. Three.

Mina cried out, arching her back.

"Shh," I soothed, leaning down to lick the pulse point at her throat. "Let him make room. You need to accommodate the team."

"It's too much," she sobbed. "You're both... you're vast."

"We are the world," I whispered against her skin. "Outside this bed, you represent chaos. Inside this bed, you are the focal point. You take everything we give you."

Rook pumped his fingers. The sound was wet, squelching. A vulgar, beautiful noise that drowned out the hum of the air conditioning.

"She's ready," Rook announced. His voice was strained, tight with the effort of holding back. "She's clamping down, but she's wet enough."

"Get out," I told him.

Rook withdrew.

I took his place.

I didn't slam into her. I couldn't. The size difference demanded precision. I held my weight on my forearms, my muscles trembling with the strain of holding back the kinetic energy stored in my frame.

I pushed the head inside.

Just the tip.

Mina screamed. A high, thin sound of being stretched beyond capacity.

"Breathe," I commanded. "Take the first inch."

I pushed harder. The tight ring of muscle fought me, then yielded. I sank in. Shallow.

The sensation was blinding. Heat. crushing pressure. Velvet friction. It was infinitely better than the dry, hard grip of a hand or the clinical function of my own palm. It felt like being swallowed by a star.

"Fuck," I roared, my head dropping to the mattress beside hers. "Rook. *Rook*."

"I see it," Rook rasped. He was hovering over us, watching the penetration with greedy eyes. "You're burying her."

"It's... tight," I ground out.

I pushed deeper. Halfway.

She was full. I could feel it. She was stretched to the limit, her body tense and vibrating.

"Mercer," she pleaded. "Please. I can't take more."

"You can," I lied. "You have to."

I withdrew almost all the way, then pushed back in. A slow, grinding stroke.

She sobbed, but her hips lifted. A biological reflex. She wanted it. The pain and the pleasure were wiring together in her brain, just as they were in mine.

"That's it," I praised. "Good girl. Good glitch."

I established a rhythm. Slow. Heavy. Inexorable. Every thrust was a statement of ownership. I wasn't just fucking her; I was printing my DNA onto her internal walls. I was ensuring that every time she closed her eyes, she would feel the phantom weight of me on top of her.

Rook couldn't just watch. He needed to be part of the connection.

He moved to her head. He knelt there, positioning himself above her face.

"Taste me," Rook ordered her. "While he stretches you. Connect the circuit."

Mina reached up. Her small hands grasped Rook's thighs. She opened her mouth.

Rook guided himself in.

Now she was full. Filled below by my cock, filled above by Rook. A conduit for our shared obsession.

I watched her face as she worked him. Her eyes fluttered shut. Her cheeks hollowed. She was servicing the monsters.

And for the first time in three years, the noise in my head stopped.

The constant strategic analysis, the rage, the competitive friction—it all went silent. There was only the wet sound of our bodies, the scent of her sugar-sweat, and the perfect, terrifying tightness of her sheath gripping me.

I reached down and interlaced my fingers with hers where they rested on the sheets. My hand engulfed hers completely.

"Ours," I claimed, driving into her as deep as I could go, hitting the cervix, making her keen around Rook's length.

Rook looked down at me. His eyes were clear. The wolf was fed.

"Ours," he agreed.

Chapter Twelve

FOREIGN TERRITORY

POV: Mina

The mattress dipped, groaning under a combined weight that felt tectonic. Mina lay paralyzed between them, feeling less like a woman and more like a specimen pinned to a slide. To her left was Mercer, a wall of icy, rigid muscle, watching her with a clinical intensity that dissected her very breath. To her right was Rook, radiating a furnace-heat, his chaotic energy vibrating against her skin like a downed power line.

They were giants. Monsters carved from scar tissue and violence who had no business looking at her—at *any* woman—with such starving, predatory focus.

Fear tasted like copper in her mouth. They were too big, too rough, too accustomed to a world where affection was just another form of wrestling. She was five feet of soft, breakable biology, and they were natural disasters. But beneath the terror, a dark, treacherous heat uncurled in her belly. She wasn't just a conquest; she was the truce. She was the soft ground where their war finally ended. The realization was intoxicating. When Mercer's heavy hand clamped possessively over her hip, and Rook's rough knuckles grazed the sensitive skin of her inner thigh, the instinct to flee dissolved, replaced by a trembling, desperate need to be ruined by them.

Mercer shifted. The movement wasn't human; it was hydraulic.

He hovered over her, his knees bracketing her hips, his weight supported on arms that looked like bridge cables. Mina couldn't look away from him. Her gaze snagged on the sharp, violent geometry of his torso. A thick vein pulsed in his neck, feeding into a shoulder scarred by years of checking men into plexiglass. His chest was a landscape of hard ridges and shallow valleys, hairless and pale, interrupted only by the jagged white line of an old surgical scar near his ribs.

He was magnificent. A terrifying masterpiece of function over form. Every inch of him was built for impact, for leverage, for dominance. And right now, that entire arsenal of aggression was aimed directly at her center.

"Don't close your eyes," Mercer commanded. His voice was a low rasp, stripping the air from the room. "Look at the logistics. Appreciate the scale."

Mina swallowed hard. "I'm looking."

"You're shaking," Rook murmured from beside her head.

He leaned over, his dark curls brushing her cheek. He smelled of rain and musk, a sharp contrast to the antiseptic scent clinging to Mercer. Rook grabbed her hand, interlacing their fingers. His palm was rough, calloused sandpaper against her smooth skin, swallowing her hand whole.

"She's scared we'll rip her," Rook told Mercer, his eyes bright with a feverish sort of delight. "Look at how small she is, Cap. She's a rounding error."

"She stretches," Mercer said. It wasn't a reassurance; it was an order to her physiology.

He adjusted his hips. The blunt, hot pressure against her entrance intensified.

Mina gasped, her back arching off the charcoal sheets. It felt impossible. He was too wide, too dense. The sheer physics of it didn't compute.

"Relax," Mercer ordered. He reached down with one hand to stroke her stomach. His thumb dug into her navel, grounding her. "You have to yield. If you fight the invasion, it hurts."

"It already hurts," she whispered.

"Good pain," Rook corrected. He brought her knuckles to his mouth, biting down lightly on the soft flesh of her hand. "Growth pain."

Mercer pushed.

He didn't slam. He sank. A slow, inexorable slide that felt like a glacier carving through a valley.

The sensation was blinding. Fire tore through her, a distinct, burning ring of stretched tissue. She cried out, a sharp, broken sound that echoed in the vast, cold room.

"Rook," Mercer gritted out, his face contorted. "Hold her down. She's twisting."

Rook moved instantly. His heavy forearm laid across her upper chest, pinning her to the mattress. Not crushing, but firm. A constraint. He lowered his face until his nose bumped hers.

"Breathe, mouse," Rook whispered. "Breathe through the nose. Let him in."

Mina squeezed her eyes shut, tears leaking from the corners. "He's too big. Please, he's splitting me."

"Open your eyes!" Mercer roared.

Her lids flew open.

Mercer was staring down at her, sweat beading on his forehead. The veins in his neck stood out in stark relief. He wasn't enjoying this in the way a normal man would. He looked like he was in agony, his jaw locked tight enough to snap teeth.

"Look at me," Mercer demanded, his voice dropping to a guttural purr. "I am holding back two hundred and forty pounds of force for you. I am vibrating with the effort of not breaking your pelvis. You will take this inch."

He drove forward. The head of his cock cleared the tightest ring of muscle.

Mina sobbed, but the burning lessened, replaced by a feeling of profound, overwhelming fullness. He was inside. He was a heavy, solid weight anchoring her to the earth.

"There," Mercer breathed, stopping. He rested his forehead against hers, his breath hot and ragged. "Hypothesis confirmed. You fit."

"Tight," Rook groaned. He was watching the junction of their bodies with obsessive fascination. "She's swallowing you, Merc. Look at that. No gap."

"No gap," Mercer agreed. He pulled back a fraction, then glided in again.

The friction was electric. It wasn't just physical; it was psychological. This was the Captain. The man on the posters. The man who had never touched a woman in his professional life. And he was burying himself inside her biology major body like it was the only home he'd ever known.

Mina's hips lifted involuntarily. Her body, traitorous and greedy, wanted more. The pain was fading into a dull throb, eclipsed by the friction of his ridges dragging against her sensitive walls.

"She likes it," Rook laughed, a dark, jagged sound. "The little freak is pushing back."

"She knows who owns her," Mercer said.

He established a rhythm. It was slow, agonizingly deliberate. He withdrew until he was almost gone, leaving her empty and cold for a heartbeat, then filled her completely in one long, devastating stroke.

Fill. Stretch. Claim.

Mina's hands scrabbled on the sheets, finding purchase on Mercer's forearms. His skin was hot, the muscles hard as iron beneath her fingers. She dug her nails in.

"Mark me," Mercer encouraged, his eyes darkening. "Draw blood. Show me you're here."

"You're doing so good, baby," Rook crooned. The endearment was shocking coming from the Enforcer, rough and clumsy but undeniably sweet. He used his free hand to wipe the tears from her temples. " taking the whole team. Such a good girl."

The praise hit her harder than the physical sensation. It bypassed her logic and went straight to the primitive part of her brain that wanted to please these monsters.

"Mercer," she gasped, her head tossing from side to side. "Deeper."

Mercer's pupils expanded, nearly swallowing the blue irises. "Greedy."

He changed the angle. He grabbed her knees and shoved them upward, pressing her thighs into her chest. It opened her completely, tilting her pelvis to accept every millimeter of him.

He drove in to the hilt.

Mina screamed, but it wasn't pain. It was a white-hot supernova of sensation. He hit something deep inside her, a spot that made her vision gray out.

"Fuck," Mercer roared, losing his clinical detachment. He slammed into her again, faster now. "Rook. Get in here."

Rook didn't need to be told twice. He crawled over her, positioning himself above her head, straddling her shoulders.

"Mouth," Rook ordered.

Mina opened for him.

He didn't hesitate. He guided himself past her lips, filling her throat just as Mercer filled her core.

She was a conduit. A bridge.

Below, Mercer's hips snapped with the precision of a piston. Above, Rook's thrusts were chaotic, eager. She was stuffed full of them, stretched tight as a drum, vibrating with their combined need.

She couldn't think. She could only feel. The roughness of Rook's hair under her fingers. The crushing weight of Mercer's chest pressing her down. The smell of male sweat and expensive soap and raw sex.

Mercer groaned, a low, animalistic sound that rumbled against her sternum.

"Rook," Mercer choked out. "Look at her. Look at where we are."

Rook pulled back slightly, breaking the seal of her mouth with a wet pop. He looked down the length of her body to where Mercer was buried inside her.

"I see it," Rook rasped. "We're plugging the leak."

"We're fixing the glitch," Mercer corrected.

He reached down between them. His large hand found the sensitive nub of her clitoris, swollen and neglected in the chaos.

He didn't rub it. He pressed his thumb down, hard.

The pressure was the catalyst.

Mina shattered.

It started in her toes, curling them tight, and rushed upward like a wildfire. Her inner muscles clamped down on Mercer, spasming violently. She tried to scream, but Rook pushed back into her mouth, stifling the sound, swallowing her cry.

"That's it," Mercer growled, his rhythm breaking into frantic, desperate chops. "Squeeze me. Milk it out of me."

He was losing it. The Captain was gone. There was only the man, starving and feral, chasing his own release inside the one thing soft enough to take it.

Rook groaned above her, his body going rigid. He pulled out of her mouth at the last second, shouting a curse as he spilled over her chin and neck, painting her skin in warm, white evidence of his surrender.

A second later, Mercer stiffened. He drove into her one last time, burying himself to the root, and held there. His entire massive frame shuddered, trembling with the force of his release. He poured into her, hot and heavy, a flood that seemed to go on forever.

Silence crashed back into the room.

The only sounds were the harsh, ragged breathing of three people and the hum of the air conditioning trying to cool the overheated space.

Mercer collapsed.

He didn't pull out. He just let his weight drop onto his elbows, careful not to crush her, but keeping her pinned. He buried his face in the curve of her neck, inhaling deeply.

"Sweet," he mumbled against her pulse point. "So sweet."

Rook slumped forward, resting his forehead on Mercer's shoulder. They formed a canopy over her, a dark, heavy tent of muscle and exhaustion.

Mina lay there, boneless. Her heart hammered against her ribs like a trapped bird. She was sticky, sore, and completely overwhelmed.

Rook's hand moved. He traced the line of her jaw, his thumb smearing the mess he'd made on her skin.

"We ruined her," Rook whispered. There was a note of awe in his voice.

Mercer lifted his head. His eyes were heavy-lidded, the blue returning to a calm, icy clarity. He looked at Mina. He looked at the flush on her chest, the bruise forming on her hip from his grip, the glazed, empty look in her eyes.

"No," Mercer said. He kissed her forehead, then turned his head to kiss Rook on the mouth—a hard, claiming press of lips that tasted of salt and Mina.

He looked back down at her, possessiveness radiating off him in waves.

"We just broke her in."

Chapter Thirteen

Worship in the Glow

POV: Mercer

My weight pinned her to the mattress.

Two hundred and forty pounds of bone and dense muscle, collapsing gravity around a girl who probably weighed less than my equipment bag. Physics dictated I should be crushing her. Biology dictated I should roll off, clean up, and sleep. That was the routine. That was the protocol Rook and I had perfected over three years of sharing beds and bodies. Friction. Release. Separation. Sleep.

I didn't move.

I couldn't.

My hips were heavy, leaden things anchored to the mattress by an exhaustion that went deeper than my muscles. I was still inside her. Not fully—the ferocity of the act had subsided into a dull, throbbing pulse—but enough to feel the terrifyingly small tremors of her inner walls fluttering against me.

She was twitching. Little spasms of aftershock traveled from her core straight into my nervous system.

Rook lay across the pillows above her head. His breathing was a wrecked, jagged sound, like a broken compressor. One of his massive arms was thrown over his eyes, shielding them from the dim light of the city bleeding through the gaps in the blackout curtains. The other hand was buried in her hair. His fingers, usually so restless, were still. He wasn't pulling. He was just holding on.

The silence in the room was absolute. No fans cheering. No scrape of skates. No shouting. Just the wet, heavy sound of our lungs working to oxygenate blood that felt too thick to pump.

Mina made a sound. A small, distressed whimper that vibrated against my sternum.

Usage.

That's what this was. We had used her. We had taken a delicate, biological anomaly and stretched it until it accommodated our violence.

I lifted my head. My neck creaked.

Her face was a mess. Mascara had smeared beneath her eyes in dark, jagged tracks where she'd cried. Her lips were swollen twice their normal size, red and abused from Rook's mouth. Her hair was a blonde disaster fanned out on the charcoal sheets, matted with sweat.

She looked wrecked.

Satisfaction, dark and oily, coated the back of my throat.

"Rook," I said. My voice was a ruin. It sounded like tires on gravel.

Rook moved his arm. He cracked one eye open. The pupil was blown wide, swallowing the iris. He looked drugged.

"Is she alive?" Rook asked. He didn't sound joking. He sounded scared.

"Check her," I ordered.

Rook shifted. He dragged his heavy body up until he was leaning over her face again. He lowered his ear to her mouth.

"Breathing," he reported. He pulled back, his expression turning strangely soft. "She smells like us. She smells like a locker room."

"She smells like the solution," I corrected.

I needed to withdraw. The logistics of the position were becoming uncomfortable. My knees dug into the mattress, and the cooling sweat on my back was starting to chill. But the thought of severing the connection made my chest tight. It wasn't logical. It was a glitch in the software.

I placed my hands on the mattress on either side of her head. I pushed up.

The friction of sliding out was agonizingly good. Slow. Dragging. Her body tried to hold onto me, a final, weak suction that nearly made my elbows buckle.

When I came free, a wet, sloppy sound echoed in the quiet room.

Mina gasped. Her eyes flew open. They were glassy, unfocused, staring up at me with zero recognition for a second before clarity slammed back in.

"Mercer," she whispered.

"Stay down," I said.

I sat back on my heels between her legs. I looked at the damage.

The sight hit me harder than a puck to the throat.

Her thighs were bruised. My fingerprints were already rising in dark angry welts on her pale skin. But the center of her...

She was gaping. A red, swollen circle where I had been. And leaking. A mix of fluids—mine, hers, Rook's—spilled out of her, coating her inner thighs, soaking into the grey sheets.

It was vulgar. It was messy. It was the most perfect thing I had ever seen.

"Look at that," I murmured.

Rook scrambled up. He crawled down the bed, ignoring personal space, ignoring dignity. He shoved his face next to my hip to see.

He made a low, wounded noise.

"We broke it," Rook said. "Cap, she's... she won't close."

"She's adjusting," I said, though my own heart rate kicked up a notch. "Elasticity. Soft tissue trauma. It recovers."

I reached out. My hand was shaking. I brushed my thumb over the inside of her knee.

"Mina."

She lifted her head weakly. She looked down the length of her body. She saw us—two giants huddled between her spread legs, staring at her ruined center like it was a holy site.

"It burns," she croaked.

"I know." I stood up. The rush of blood from my head made the room spin. "Stay. Do not move."

I walked to the en-suite. The cold tile shocked the soles of my feet. I grabbed a washcloth from the stack—white, fluffy, pristine. I ran it under warm water. Not hot. Just tepid.

I looked at myself in the mirror above the sink.

I didn't recognize the man staring back.

My hair was standing on end. My lips were bitten and bloody. There were scratch marks on my pectorals—small, crescent-moon indentations where she had tried to find purchase while I tore her apart.

But it was the eyes.

The ice was gone. The calculation was gone. There was just a flat, terrifying possessiveness. I looked like a man who had found the one thing he would kill to keep.

I turned off the tap. I squeezed the cloth.

When I returned to the bedroom, Rook hadn't moved. He was still kneeling between her ankles, his hands hovering over her legs, afraid to touch.

"Move," I said.

Rook shifted back, giving me space but refusing to leave the bed.

I knelt. I took her left leg and draped it over my shoulder to open her up again. She hissed, her hands gripping the sheets.

"Quiet," I ordered softly. "Maintenance."

I pressed the warm cloth to her.

She flinched violently, her hips bucking off the mattress.

"Easy." I used my free hand to flatten her stomach, holding her down. "I've got you. It cleans the wound."

I wiped her. The white cloth turned pink and grey. I was gentle—or as gentle as hands like mine could be. I cleaned the inner thighs. I dabbed at the swollen entrance. I wiped away the evidence of Rook's earlier claim from her stomach.

She watched me. Her grey eyes were wide, lucid now. She wasn't looking at me with fear anymore. She was looking at me with confusion.

"You're... cleaning me," she whispered.

"Infection risk," I stated. "Hygiene is critical for recovery."

"You're the Captain," she said, as if that explained why I shouldn't be wiping fluids off a biology student's thighs.

"I am handling my asset," I said.

I tossed the dirty cloth onto the floor.

"Rook," I said. "Hydration."

Rook nodded. He rolled off the bed. He was naked, shameless, his body a map of scars and defined muscle. He walked to the mini-fridge in the corner and grabbed three bottles of water.

He cracked two open before he even turned around, downing one in a single, long swallow. He brought the other two to the bed.

He handed one to Mina.

"Drink," Rook said. He sat on the edge of the mattress, his hip pressing against her shoulder. "Replace the fluids."

Mina struggled to sit up. Her arms trembled, too weak to support her weight.

Rook made a tutting sound. He reached out, curled a massive arm around her waist, and hauled her up. He pulled her back until she was resting against his chest.

She looked tiny against him. A child's doll propped up against a tank.

She drank. Water spilled down her chin. Rook caught it with his thumb, smearing it over her lower lip, his eyes dark and hungry again.

"Greedy," Rook muttered. "She

Chapter Fourteen

The Sweetest Intrusion

POV: Mina

Mercer's charcoal hoodie swallowed me. The hem brushed my knees, the cuffs completely engulfed my hands, and the neckline slid off one shoulder, exposing the mottled bruise Rook had left there with his mouth hours ago.

Standing in the center of the kitchen, surrounded by brushed steel and black marble, the absurdity of my existence magnified. This space was designed for giants. The cabinets hovered out of reach. The island counter hit me at the ribcage. The air smelled of ozone, filtered cleanliness, and the faint, lingering musk of two men who had spent the night tearing me apart and putting me back together.

Sunlight sliced through the floor-to-ceiling windows. It wasn't the soft, golden light of the dorms. This was hard, high-altitude light, illuminating the dust motes dancing over the expensive espresso machine.

My body hummed with a deep, persistent ache. Not pain, exactly. *Awareness.* My inner thighs throbbed with a dull, heavy pulse that synced with my heartbeat. Every step sent a jolt of sensation shooting upward, a constant, visceral reminder of the dual invasion I had accepted.

I reached for the cabinet handle to get a mug. My fingers grazed the cool metal, but the shelf was too high. I stretched, rising onto my tiptoes, the hoodie riding up my thighs.

A large, warm hand clamped over my waist.

Gravity shifted.

"Don't climb," Mercer's voice rumbled against my ear. "You break too easily."

He didn't lift me. He pinned me to the counter. His chest pressed against my back, a wall of solid heat transferring through the thick cotton of the hoodie. He reached up, his arm extending effortlessly over my head to grab a white ceramic mug.

He set it on the counter but didn't pull away. He boxed me in, his hands gripping the marble edge on either side of my hips.

"Morning," he murmured.

He sounded different. The sharp, military cadence was gone, replaced by something rougher. Sleep-heavy. Or maybe just satisfied.

I turned in the cage of his arms.

Mercer wore nothing but low-slung grey sweatpants. His torso was a landscape of pale, corded muscle and old scars. But my eyes snagged on the fresh marks. scratches on his pectorals. A bite mark on his traps.

I did that.

Mercer caught me staring. His mouth didn't curve into a smile—that would be too human—but his eyes, usually icy and remote, burned with a terrifying blue intensity. He reached out and tugged the hood of the sweatshirt up, covering my messy hair, framing my face in dark fabric.

"You look ridiculous," he said softly.

"It's too big," I whispered.

"It's correct," he countered. He ran a thumb over my lower lip, pressing down until my mouth opened slightly. "It marks the territory. Anyone who sees you in this knows you belong to the Captain."

"Nobody is going to see me," I argued, though the fight in my voice was pathetic. "I have to change to go to campus."

"Campus." He said the word like it was a dirty joke. "Rook thinks we should keep you here. Lock the doors. Order in."

"I have a lab at two."

"We bought the building," Mercer said simply. "We could condemn it."

My heart stuttered. He wasn't joking. The scary part wasn't the threat; it was the realization that I wanted him to do it. I wanted to be locked in this high-tower fortress, safe from the noise, safe from the loneliness, existing only as a pet for two monsters.

Heavy footsteps thudded on the hardwood.

Rook appeared in the archway. He was less composed than Mercer. His dark hair stood up in wild curls, and he hadn't bothered with pants. He wore boxer briefs that left absolutely nothing to the imagination.

He stopped dead when he saw me.

His eyes tracked from my bare feet up to the oversized hoodie, lingering on the way the fabric draped over my curves. His pupils expanded until his eyes were almost black.

"Fuck," Rook breathed. "Merc, look at the mouse."

"I'm looking," Mercer said, not moving an inch.

Rook crossed the kitchen in three long strides. He didn't ask for permission. He crowded into the space, pressing against my side, sandwiching me between them. He wrapped a heavy arm around my waist and buried his face in the crook of my neck, inhaling deeply.

"Sugar," Rook groaned against my skin. "And us. Mostly us."

He nipped the sensitive cord of my neck.

"Did you feed her?" Rook asked, pulling back to look at Mercer. "She needs fuel. We depleted the reserves."

"I'm making coffee," Mercer said. He turned to the machine, his movements precise and efficient. "Sit her up."

Rook grabbed me under the arms and lifted me like a toddler. He deposited me onto the marble counter. The stone chilled the back of my thighs, but the heat radiating from Rook kept me from shivering. He stepped between my knees, forcing them apart, settling into the space he had claimed last night.

He ran his large, rough hands up my calves, checking the skin.

"Bruises," Rook noted, tracing a dark mark on my inner thigh with his thumb. His voice dropped, losing its playful edge. "My grip. Too hard."

"It doesn't hurt," I lied.

"Liar." Rook leaned in, pressing his forehead against mine. "It hurts. But you like it. You like knowing who was there."

"Rook," Mercer warned from the machine. "Don't agitate the specimen before caffeine."

Mercer turned around. He held a mug.

He didn't hand it to me. He brought it to his own lips, blew on it softly, and then held it to my mouth.

"Drink," Mercer ordered.

I took a sip. It was perfect. Rich, dark, but sweetened exactly how I liked it. He had memorized my preference from one interaction at the gala.

"Good?" Mercer asked, watching my throat work.

"Yes."

He set the mug down and picked up a silver spoon from the counter. It held a single, sugar-dusted strawberry.

"Open," he commanded.

I parted my lips. Mercer slid the spoon into my mouth. The sweetness of the fruit exploded on my tongue, but I could barely taste it over the intensity of his gaze. He watched my mouth close around the metal, his eyes darkening. He looked like he wanted to be the spoon.

"Sweet thing," Rook murmured, watching from inches away. "Look at her eat. She's so..."

"Delicate," Mercer finished. "Fragile architecture."

He reached out and used his thumb to wipe a drop of red juice from the corner of my lip. He put the thumb in his own mouth, sucking it clean while holding my gaze.

The air in the kitchen thickened, turning heavy and charged. This wasn't domestic bliss. This was a predator playing with its food before the kill.

"About the schedule," Mercer said, his voice dropping into business mode, though his hand drifted to rest on my knee. "We practiced the integration last night. The physical compatibility is... exceptional."

"Exceptional?" Rook snorted. "Merc, we fit like a plug in a socket. Better."

"However," Mercer continued, ignoring him. "The emotional containment needs work. You were leaking."

My face heated. "I was overwhelmed."

"You were crying," Mercer corrected. "You were sobbing my name while Rook had his hand in your mouth."

"So?" Rook defended me, his hands tightening on my thighs. "It was a lot. We're a lot."

"It creates a vulnerability," Mercer said. He stepped closer, wedging himself next to Rook so they formed a solid wall of male muscle in front of me. "If you cry, we stop thinking. When you made that sound—the high one, when I bottomed out—my tactical brain shut down. I would have burned the city to the ground to make it stop. Or make it happen again. I couldn't tell which."

Mercer looked at me, his expression terrifyingly serious.

"You compromise our defenses, Mina. You make us irrational."

"I can leave," I whispered.

The reaction was instantaneous.

Rook growled—a low, animalistic rumble in his chest. Mercer's hand snapped out, gripping my chin, tilting my head back until my neck was exposed.

"Incorrect," Mercer hissed. "You don't leave. You adjust. We adjust."

"We need the buffer," Rook said, his voice urgent. "You saw the game tapes. You saw us fighting. Last night? I slept for six hours. Dreamless. No rage. No noise. Just... quiet."

He took my hand, pressing it flat against his chest, right over his heart. It beat steady and strong under my palm.

"You did that," Rook said. "You're the quiet."

I looked at them. Two apex predators, the gods of the campus, the kings of the ice. They had everything. Money, fame, each other. And yet they were looking at me—the girl who sat in the back of the lecture hall and rescued stray cats—like I was the only water source in a desert.

"So I'm a pacifier," I said, testing the boundaries.

"You're a necessity," Mercer corrected. He released my chin but kept his hand on my neck, his thumb resting on my pulse. "Like oxygen. Like gravity. We don't have to like needing it. We just do."

"Do you like it?" I asked. "Or do you just tolerate the biology?"

Mercer went still. He studied my face, cataloging every freckle, every lash.

"I tolerate the biology," he said clinically. "I tolerate the noise of women. The softness. The inefficiency."

He leaned in closer.

"But you..." He brushed his nose against mine. "I am obsessed with the exception. I want to take you apart and see why you work."

"And put me back together?"

"Eventually," he murmured. "After we've memorized the pieces."

Rook grew impatient with the talking. He leaned in and bit the soft skin of my shoulder through the hoodie.

"Stop analyzing her, Cap. Look at her legs." Rook's hand slid higher, dangerously close to the hem of the sweatshirt. "We should put her back in bed. We have morning practice in two hours. That's enough time for a maintenance round."

"She's sore," Mercer noted, though he didn't stop Rook's hand.

"She heals fast," Rook argued. "And we can be gentle. Use the oil this time. No stretching. just... friction."

"Just friction," Mercer repeated the lie we had established at the start.

But as he looked at me, as his thumb stroked the pulse point in my neck, I knew it wasn't just friction. Friction didn't look at you like you were a holy relic. Friction didn't clean you up with warm water and wrap you in jerseys to keep you warm.

"I have class," I said weakly.

"Skip it," Rook suggested against my neck.

"No," Mercer said. He pulled back, establishing command again. "She goes to class. She maintains her routine. If we isolate her completely, the stress variables increase. She needs her little life."

Her little life. As if everything outside of this penthouse was just a hobby to keep me occupied until they needed me again.

"But," Mercer added, his eyes narrowing. "You wear the hoodie."

"To class?" I asked, horrified. "It's huge. It has your name on the back."

"Exactly," Mercer said. "You wear it. You sit in the front row. And if anyone asks why you're wearing the Captain's gear, you tell them..."

He paused, a cruel, possessive smile touching his lips.

"...you tell them you were cold."

Rook laughed, the sound vibrating against my ribs. "Territorial bastard. I love it."

"Off the counter," Mercer ordered. "Go change into leggings. Keep the hoodie. We're driving you."

"I can walk."

"You waddle," Rook pointed out, grinning. "We did a number on your gait, mouse. You're not walking anywhere without us."

He helped me down. My feet hit the floor, and my knees buckled slightly. Rook caught me instantly, hauling me against his chest.

For a moment, I just let myself hang there, supported by his massive strength. I breathed in his scent—cedar and sweat—and felt a wave of terrifying comfort wash over me.

This was wrong. It was toxic. It was a codependent spiral with two men who viewed affection as a weakness to be drilled out of their systems.

But as Rook held me up and Mercer watched me with that starving, reverent gaze, the logic centers of my brain went quiet. I didn't care about the hypothesis anymore. I didn't care about the variables.

I just liked being the soft thing that kept the monsters from eating each other.

"Okay," I whispered into Rook's chest. "Drive me."

Mercer reached out and smoothed the hair from my face.

"Good girl," he said. "Now go cover those legs before I decide the lecture hall can wait."

I turned and walked toward the bedroom to find my leggings. I didn't look back, but I could feel their eyes on me. A physical weight. A tether.

"Eight hours," I heard Rook mutter behind me. "We have to wait eight hours to touch her again? That's bullshit."

"We'll survive," Mercer replied, though his voice sounded strained. "We have the game tonight. We need the aggression."

"If we lose," Rook threatened, "I'm taking it out on her."

"If we win," Mercer countered, "I'm taking it out on her."

I paused in the doorway, my hand on the frame. A shiver that had nothing to do with cold and everything to do with anticipation prickled across my skin.

Win or lose. Rage or celebration.

I was the destination.

I walked into the dark bedroom, stripped off the hoodie for just a second to pull on my leggings, and caught my reflection in the mirror.

My lips were red. My eyes were bright. I looked like a woman who had been thoroughly, devastatingly worshipped.

I pulled the hoodie back on, drowning in Mercer's scent, and smiled.

Let them play their game. I knew where the real victory was. It was waiting for them right here, soft and warm and ready to break their fall.

Chapter Fifteen

THE BIOLOGICAL OVERRIDE

POV: Mina

The tunnel outside the locker room smelled of ammonia, damp equipment, and defeat. It was a sharp, chemical stink that coated the back of the throat.

I stood near the security barrier, my hands buried deep in the kangaroo pocket of Mercer's charcoal hoodie. The fabric engulfed me, the hem hitting the tops of my knees, but it offered zero protection against the sub-zero chill radiating from the concrete walls.

Or maybe the cold came from the team.

The double doors swung open. The silence was absolute. No music. No shouting. Just the heavy, rhythmic thud of boots and the rasp of equipment bags dragging on the floor.

They lost. 3-2 in overtime. A sloppy goal that slipped past the goalie while Mercer was in the penalty box for fighting and Rook was busy trying to detach an opponent's head from his shoulders.

The air pressure in the corridor dropped.

Mercer appeared first.

He wore a suit that cost more than my tuition, but he looked like he'd been in a car wreck. His tie hung loose around an unbuttoned collar. His hair, usually slicked back with military precision, fell in damp, chaotic strands over his forehead. A distinct, purple bruise bloomed high on his cheekbone, vivid against his pale skin.

He didn't look like a captain. He looked like a weapon that had misfired.

He stopped when he saw me.

He didn't smile. The blue of his eyes was gone, swallowed by a dilated, black rage. He looked at me—really looked at me—but it wasn't the worshipful gaze of this morning. It was cold. Distant. He looked at me like I was a civilian standing in the middle of a blast zone.

"Car," Mercer clipped out. He didn't break stride. He walked right past me, the wind of his movement smelling of expensive soap and violence.

Rook followed a second later.

He looked worse. His lip was split, a jagged red line crusted with dried blood. His knuckles were raw. He radiated heat, a furnace of agitation that made the air around him ripple.

He saw me and halted. His chest heaved. He took a step toward me, his hand twitching at his side like he wanted to reach out, to grab the hoodie and drag me against him. His nostrils flared, inhaling the scent of me, searching for the sugar and softness he claimed to need.

Then he stopped. He looked at his own hand—bruised, swollen, shaking with adrenaline—and then at my neck.

"Don't," Rook growled. It sounded like a warning to himself. "Don't look at us, mouse. Not tonight."

He shoved past me, following Mercer's wake.

The rejection hit me in the chest, a physical blow that knocked the breath out of my lungs.

The bad habits.

They were doing it. The thing they warned me about. The thing the sports blogs gossiped about. When they lost, they shut down. They turned inward, feeding on each other's rage, locking out the rest of the world because nothing soft could survive their atmosphere.

I should have stayed at the dorm. I should have let them decompose in their penthouse alone.

But my feet were already moving. I jogged to catch up, my sneakers squeaking on the concrete, chasing the two monsters who were currently trying to run away from their own pet.

*

The ride to the penthouse was a study in suffocation.

Mercer drove. His hands strangled the leather steering wheel, his knuckles white. The veins in his forearms stood out like ridges on a topographic map, tracing the line of muscle from wrist to elbow.

I sat in the back. The partition was down, but the silence built a wall thicker than glass.

I watched Mercer in the rearview mirror. I couldn't help it. Even in this state—cold, furious, shutting me out—the sheer architecture of the man ruined me. The way his deltoids strained the seams of his jacket as he took a sharp turn. The thick, corded column of his neck. He was terrifying, yes, but it was the kind of terror that made my mouth water. He was a masterpiece of masculine aggression, a creature designed for impact. I wanted to climb over the center console. I wanted to wrap myself around those shoulders and force him to feel something other than the loss.

I wanted to bite that vein in his neck until he stopped staring at the road and looked at me.

Rook sat in the passenger seat, staring out the window. He was vibrating. His leg bounced a frantic rhythm. He wasn't looking at the city; he was replaying the game, every missed check, every lost puck.

We pulled into the underground garage. The engine cut.

"Go upstairs," Mercer said. He didn't turn around. "Go to the guest room. Lock the door."

"I sleep in your room," I said. My voice sounded small in the expansive leather interior, but I forced it steady.

"Not tonight," Rook snapped. He opened his door and slammed it shut, the sound echoing like a gunshot.

I scrambled out. They were already walking toward the elevator, two towering shadows moving in sync. I ran to the closing doors and slipped my hand between the sensors.

The doors jerked back open.

Mercer glared down at me. "Mina. I gave you an order."

"I'm not a rookie," I said, stepping inside. I pressed my back against the metal wall, looking up at them. "And I'm not a fan. You don't get to dismiss me because you had a bad day."

"A bad day?" Mercer let out a harsh, dry laugh. He loomed over me, planting a hand on the wall next to my head. "We didn't have a bad day. We failed. The unit broke down. And right now, the only thing I want to do is tear something apart to see if it fixes the noise in my head."

He leaned closer, his scent overpowering—musk, cedar, and the metallic tang of adrenaline.

"You are soft," Mercer whispered, his voice dripping with a cruel sort of reverence. "You are breakable. If you come into that apartment with us, we aren't going to braid your hair. We are going to use you to purge this. And it won't be gentle."

"I didn't ask you to be gentle," I whispered back.

Mercer's eyes widened slightly. A flicker of blue cut through the black.

Rook made a noise in his throat—half groan, half snarl.

The elevator dinged. The doors opened directly into the penthouse.

They stormed out. They didn't turn on the lights. The city glow from the floor-to-ceiling windows cast long, distorted shadows across the furniture.

Rook ripped his jacket off and threw it on the floor. He paced the length of the living room, tearing at his shirt buttons until they popped, scattering like hail on the hardwood.

"I need to hit something," Rook muttered. He turned to Mercer. "Center ice. Third period. You hesitated."

"I was positioning," Mercer shot back, stripping off his own jacket with meticulous, angry movements. "You missed the check. You let him skate right by you."

"I was covering your ass!" Rook roared. He shoved Mercer.

Mercer shoved back. Hard.

Rook stumbled, hitting the back of the sofa. He rebounded instantly, launching himself at Mercer. They collided with a meaty thud, grappling, snarling like wolves fighting over a carcass. It wasn't a fight—it was a ritual. A violent, physical language they had spoken for years.

I stood by the elevator, watching.

It should have been frightening. Two giants, six-foot-six and built like tanks, tearing at each other in the semi-darkness. But it wasn't fear that pooled in my belly. It was heat.

They were starving. They were trying to bleed out the failure.

"Stop," I said.

My voice was soft, but in the cavernous room, it acted like a gunshot.

They froze. Mercer had Rook pinned against the wall, his forearm pressed against Rook's throat. Rook's hand was fisted in Mercer's shirt. They were chest to chest, panting, their foreheads touching.

They turned their heads slowly to look at me.

"Leave the room, Mina," Mercer warned. His voice was ragged.

I walked toward them.

I didn't run. I didn't flinch. I walked across the expensive rug, stepping over the discarded jackets, until I was standing right next to them.

I was tiny. The top of my head barely reached Mercer's chest. I looked up at the tangle of limbs and rage.

"You're not fighting," I observed calmly. "You're panicking."

"We don't panic," Rook spat, though his grip on Mercer loosened.

"You do," I said. "You're scared you're not good enough. So you're trying to hurt him before the world hurts you."

I reached out.

I placed my hand flat on Mercer's chest, right over his heart. It hammered against my palm, a frantic, erratic bird.

"You're leaking," I said, using Mercer's own word against him. "Inefficient."

Mercer looked down at my hand. His eyes traced the small, pale fingers splayed against his dark shirt. He trembled. The violence in him was vibrating against my skin, looking for a conductor.

"If you touch us right now," Mercer rasped, "we will ruin you."

"Try," I dared him.

The air snapped.

Mercer released Rook. In the same motion, his hand clamped around my throat. Not squeezing—never squeezing—but holding. Claiming. His thumb rested on my windpipe, feeling the swallow, feeling the trust.

"Rook," Mercer said, his eyes never leaving mine. "The couch."

Rook didn't argue. He didn't hesitate. He grabbed me from behind, his arms wrapping around my waist, lifting me off the floor like I weighed nothing.

"Mine," Rook growled into my ear. "My turn. My rage."

He carried me to the massive leather sectional and threw me down. I bounced on the cushions, scrambling to look up.

They towered over me. The moonlight caught the sweat on their skin, the blood on Rook's lip, the bruise on Mercer's cheek. They stripped the rest of their clothes off with frantic, tearing motions. Belt buckles clattered. Zippers hissed.

When they were naked, they were terrifying. Massive. Hard. Ready for war.

Mercer crawled onto the couch, caging me between his arms. Usually, he asked. Usually, he calibrated.

Tonight, there was no calibration.

"You wanted this," Mercer snarled, dragging my leggings down my legs in one ruthless swipe. "You wanted the monsters."

"Yes," I breathed.

"Then take them."

Mercer didn't wait. He didn't prep me. He used the slick heat of my own desire and shoved into me.

I screamed.

It wasn't pain—okay, it was a little pain—but mostly it was the sheer, overwhelming fullness of him. He filled every corner of me, stretching me, grounding me.

Rook was there instantly. He didn't wait for an invitation. He knelt behind the couch, grabbing my hair, tilting my head back.

"Look at me," Rook demanded.

I looked up, upside down, into his wild, dark eyes.

"You don't leave," Rook said fierce and broken. "When we lose, you don't leave. You stay. You take it."

He crashed his mouth onto mine.

He tasted of blood and copper. He kissed me like he was trying to breathe through me.

I wasn't just a stress ball. I wasn't just a hole. I was the anchor. I was the only thing heavy enough to hold them to the earth when their own gravity failed.

I wrapped my legs around Mercer's waist, pulling him deeper, forcing him to feel the softness he laid siege to. I grabbed Rook's hair, pulling him closer.

"I'm here," I sobbed into Rook's mouth, while Mercer pounded the truth of it into my body. "I'm right here."

The coldness vanished. The distance evaporated. There was only heat, sweat, and the desperate, sickeningly sweet realization that they couldn't survive the fall without me to catch them.

Chapter Sixteen

Reinstating the Ban

POV: Mina

I woke up drowning.

Not in water, but in heat. In weight. In the terrifying, suffocating density of male affection.

My face was pressed into the junction of a shoulder and a pectoral muscle—hard, hairless, smelling of sandalwood and the unique, iron-tang of Mercer's skin. A heavy arm, thick as a tree branch, lay draped across my waist, pinning me to the mattress.

I tried to shift. The arm tightened instantly. A reflex. A bear trap snapping shut.

"Still," a voice rumbled from above. "She's waking up."

"Check the temperature," another voice whispered, rough with sleep. Rook. "She feels cool. Is the AC too high?"

"Her circulation is poor. Small extremities."

I cracked my eyes open.

The world was a wall of flesh. Mercer lay on his back, acting as my pillow. Rook was curled around my other side, his massive frame effectively acting as a secondary duvet. I was the filling in a sandwich made of two hundred and forty-pound NHL players.

I looked up.

Mercer wasn't sleeping. He was watching me. His blue eyes were terrifyingly clear, devoid of the exhaustion that should have been there after last night's game and the subsequent... activity. He looked like a scientist observing a rare, volatile compound.

Rook propped himself up on an elbow. He reached out, his large hand hovering over my face before landing on my forehead. His palm swallowed my entire field of vision.

"No fever," Rook reported to Mercer. He looked down at me, his dark eyes melting into a sweet, gooey expression that looked bizarre on his scarred face. "Morning, sugar. Did we crush you?"

"I can't breathe," I whispered.

"Good," Mercer said. He didn't move. He actually pressed me closer, his hand coming up to cup the back of my head, forcing my nose against his neck. "Oxygen is secondary. Proximity is primary."

"Mercer," I mumbled into his skin. "I need to pee."

"Hold it," Rook said. He nuzzled his face into my hair, inhaling deeply. "Five more minutes. We need to recharge. You're the battery."

This was it. This was the "morning after" I had dreaded, but it wasn't cold. It wasn't the icy dismissal I had prepared my heart for.

It was worse.

It was a siege.

They weren't pushing me away because they had lost the game; they were burying themselves inside me to hide from the failure. I was their bunker.

I pushed against Mercer's chest. It was like pushing a granite slab. "I really need to get up."

Mercer sighed—a long, suffering sound. He released his grip on my head. "Fine. Rook, escort."

"On it."

Rook rolled off the bed. He was naked, glorious, and completely unbothered by the morning light streaming through the gaps in the curtains. He scooped me up out of the sheets before I could even swing my legs over the edge.

"I can walk," I protested, my voice small in the cavernous room.

"Why walk when you can fly?" Rook grinned. He kissed my nose. Then my cheek. Then my chin. Quick, peppering kisses that felt manic. "Our little bird. Our good luck charm. We're never losing a game again, you know that? We figured out the variable."

He carried me to the bathroom and set me down on the plush rug. He didn't leave. He leaned against the doorframe, arms crossed, watching.

"Privacy?" I asked, clutching my oversized t-shirt—Mercer's t-shirt—to my thighs.

"Unnecessary," Rook said. "We've been inside you, Mina. We've mapped every inch. Mystery is inefficient."

I closed the door in his face. He didn't leave. I could see his shadow under the door. I could hear him humming.

My hands shook as I washed my face. The mirror showed a girl who looked thoroughly, devastatingly loved. My lips were swollen. rub burn marked my neck. My hair was a bird's nest.

But inside, the panic was rising. A cold, black tide.

They didn't see *me*. They saw a cure. They saw a stress ball that breathed.

When I came out, they were waiting. Both of them. Mercer had put on sweatpants, but his chest remained bare. He held a tray.

"Breakfast," Mercer announced. "High protein. Complex carbohydrates. We need to build your endurance."

He walked past me, back to the bed, and set the tray down. It was laden with eggs, fruit, toast, and coffee. Enough food for a linebacker.

"Get in," Mercer ordered, patting the mattress.

"I have to go to class," I said. I stayed by the door. "I have a lab at ten."

Mercer and Rook exchanged a look. A knowing, patronizing look that adults give a toddler asking for a pony.

"About that," Mercer said. He sat on the edge of the bed, spreading his legs, looking like a king on a throne. "We discussed the logistics while you were sleeping."

"Logistics?"

"The commute," Rook explained, bouncing on his heels. "It's wasteful. And the stress of your coursework? It releases cortisol. Cortisol makes your scent sour. We don't like sour."

"So," Mercer continued, buttering a piece of toast with precise, surgical strokes. "We decided it's best if you take a sabbatical."

The air left the room.

"A what?"

"A break," Mercer said calmly. "We looked at your syllabus. It's rigorous. Unnecessary. You don't need the degree, Mina. You have us. We have resources. You'll stay here, manage the household, manage *us*. It's a full-time position."

My mouth opened, but no sound came out.

They had decided. They had sat there, watching me sleep, and decided to erase my future because my stress smelled bad to them.

"I can't just quit school," I said, my voice rising. "I'm a biology major. I have a scholarship."

"We'll pay it off," Rook waved a hand dismissively. He walked over to me, looming, crowding my space with his heat. He reached out to stroke my hair. "Money is paper, mouse. We have mountains of it. What we don't have... is peace. You give us peace."

He lifted a strand of my blonde hair, wrapping it around his thick, scarred finger. A golden chain.

"We want to keep you," Rook whispered, his eyes dark and dilated. "Wrapped in cotton. Safe. Right here where we can smell you."

"You're talking about a prison," I said.

"A palace," Mercer corrected. He held out the buttered toast. "Come here. Eat. You're trembling. Low blood sugar."

"I'm trembling because you're insane!"

The shout echoed off the high ceilings.

Mercer lowered the toast. His face didn't twist in anger. It smoothed out into a mask of confused concern. He looked at Rook, then back at me.

"We are offering you everything," Mercer state slowly. "Protection. Comfort. Worship. We treat you like a queen."

"You treat me like a pet!" I cried. Tears pricked my eyes—angry, hot tears. "You decided my life while I was sleeping! You don't want a girlfriend. You don't even want a partner. You want a... a emotional support animal that you can fuck."

Rook flinched. The hurt on his face was genuine, which made it worse. He looked like a kicked puppy. A six-foot-six, two-hundred-and-forty-pound puppy capable of murder.

"That's not fair," Rook mumbled. "We love you."

"You love how I make you feel," I corrected. "There's a difference."

I turned to the closet. My clothes were gone.

I spun around. "Where are my clothes?"

"Donated," Mercer said. He stood up now, his presence filling the room. "They were cheap polyester. Irritants to the skin. I ordered replacements. Silk. Cashmere. They arrive at noon."

"My jeans," I demanded. "My sneakers."

"Gone," Mercer said. "We are upgrading you."

Panic clawed at my throat. It wasn't just the clothes. It was the erasure. They were systematically removing every trace of Mina the Student and replacing her with Mina the Consort.

I scanned the room. On the floor, near the door, lay the pile of yesterday's clothes. My leggings. The oversized hoodie I had worn to the game.

I dove for them.

"Mina, stop," Mercer commanded. It was his captain's voice. The one that made rookies freeze on the ice.

I didn't freeze. I scrambled into the leggings, hopping on one foot, my heart hammering a frantic rhythm against my ribs.

Rook moved to intercept me. "Mouse, don't. You're upset. Let us fix it. Come back to bed. We'll make you come. You always think clearer after."

"No!" I jerked away from his reaching hand.

Rook froze, looking at his empty hand as if I had burned it.

I pulled the hoodie over my head. It smelled of them. It engulfed me. Even trying to leave, I was wearing their skin.

"I'm leaving," I said. My voice broke. "I'm going to the dorms."

"You can't," Mercer said. He walked toward me. He didn't run. He moved with the inevitable momentum of a glacier. "You don't fit there anymore. You've expanded. You need us."

"I need to be a person," I sobbed. "I need to study cells under a microscope, not be the specimen under yours."

I backed toward the elevator.

Mercer stopped. He stood in the center of the room, flanked by Rook. Two titans. Two gods. They looked beautiful and tragic and terrifying.

"If you walk out that door," Mercer said softly, "we won't chase you."

It was a lie. I could see the muscles in his legs twitching, ready to spring. He was using every ounce of his discipline to keep from tackling me and dragging me back to the nest.

"Good," I lied back.

"We give you everything," Rook pleaded, tears swimming in his eyes. "Why isn't it enough?"

"Because it's too much," I whispered. "It's eating me alive."

I hit the call button. The doors opened immediately.

I stepped inside.

The last thing I saw before the metal doors slid shut was Mercer grabbing Rook's arm to stop him from charging, and Rook burying his face in his hands. They looked like statues of grief.

The doors closed.

The silence in the elevator was worse than the noise.

I wrapped my arms around myself, burying my hands in the pocket of Mercer's hoodie. My fingers brushed against something hard.

I pulled it out.

It was a black velvet box.

My breath hitched. I flipped it open.

Inside wasn't a ring. It was a key. A heavy, old-fashioned iron key on a platinum chain. And a note, written in Mercer's sharp, architectural handwriting.

The East Wing. For your laboratory. We bought the equipment.

A sob tore out of my throat, harsh and ugly.

They had bought me a lab. inside the house. So I could work without leaving them.

It was the sweetest, sickest thing I had ever seen.

I shoved the box back into the pocket and leaned my head against the cool metal wall. I had to get out. I had to get away.

Because the terrifying truth wasn't that I hated their cage.

The truth was, I was already looking for the key to lock myself back in.

*

The campus library was a tomb of dust and silence.

I sat at a back table, buried behind a fortress of textbooks I wasn't reading. The fluorescent lights hummed—a cheap, buzzing sound compared to the silent, expensive air of the penthouse.

It had been eight hours.

My phone sat on the table, face down. It hadn't vibrated. Not once.

We won't chase you.

Mercer was a man of his word. A cruel, precise man. He was letting me feel the cold. He knew that after the furnace of their attention, the real world would feel like an ice bath.

He was right.

I felt phantom touches everywhere. The ghost of a heavy hand on my thigh. The memory of Rook's breath on my neck. My skin felt too loose, like it was trying to detach itself from my body because it wasn't being held together by their grip.

"Is this seat taken?"

I jumped.

A guy stood there. Normal height. Maybe five-ten. Brown hair. Blandly handsome. He wore a generic university sweatshirt.

"No," I croaked. My voice was rusty.

He sat down. He smiled. It was a nice smile. Safe. "I'm Kevin. Civ-E major. I've seen you in the Science building."

"Mina," I said automatically.

"I know," Kevin said. "You're the girl who rescued the kitten from the drain last month. That was cool."

He was flirting. A normal, human interaction.

I stared at him. I tried to find him attractive. I tried to appreciate the symmetry of his face, the kindness in his eyes.

But all I could see was what he lacked.

He wasn't a giant. He didn't smell like a storm. He didn't look at me like he wanted to devour me whole and keep the bones. He looked at me like I was a girl he wanted to buy a coffee.

It felt... flavorless.

"Are you okay?" Kevin asked, leaning in slightly. "You look a little... intense."

"I'm fine," I said.

I looked down at my notes. *Cellular Mitosis.* The division of cells. Splitting apart to create new life.

"You're wearing a Man Advantage hoodie," Kevin noted, pointing to my chest. "Mercer's number. Big fan?"

The name went through me like a spear.

"My boyfriend's," I said. The word tasted bland. *Boyfriend.* It felt woefully inadequate to describe the monsters.

"Oh." Kevin's face fell slightly. "Lucky guy. Mercer is a beast. Total psychopath on the ice, though. Did you see him last night? Almost killed a guy."

"He protects his team," I said sharply. The defense was instinctual.

"Sure," Kevin laughed nervously. "If you like that sort of thing. Personally, I think he compensates. Too much aggression usually means—"

The air pressure in the library dropped.

The hair on my arms stood up. Not a shiver. A biological alert system.

The silence in the library changed. It wasn't the quiet of study anymore. It was the quiet of prey sensing a predator.

I smelled it before I saw them.

Cedar. Musk. Ozone.

I looked up.

Standing at the end of the aisle, blocking the exit, were two figures.

They weren't wearing suits. They weren't wearing hockey gear. They were wearing black jeans and black t-shirts that strained across their chests.

Rook was vibrating. His hands were opening and closing at his sides. His eyes were locked on Kevin like a missile guidance system acquiring a target.

Mercer stood perfectly still. He was a statue of judgment. His gaze moved from Kevin, to me, to the distance between us.

Kevin followed my gaze. He turned around.

"Holy shit," Kevin whispered. "Is that..."

Mercer took a step forward.

He didn't look at Kevin. He looked at me.

"We lied," Mercer said.

His voice wasn't loud, but it carried through the stacks like a command from god.

"We tried," Rook added, stepping up beside him. His voice was wrecked, raw. "We stayed in the apartment for eight hours. We stared at the door."

"We realized something," Mercer said, walking down the aisle.

Students were looking up now. Whispers started. Phones came out. The Kings of Campus were invading the nerd sanctuary.

Mercer didn't care. He stopped three feet away from the table. He ignored Kevin completely. Kevin shrank back, pressing himself into his chair, realizing he was suddenly a very small animal in a very dangerous jungle.

"What did you realize?" I whispered.

Mercer leaned down. He placed his hands on the table, leaning into my space.

"That we don't care about your autonomy," Mercer said darkly. "We don't care about your degree. We don't care about fairness."

"We tried to be noble," Rook rasped, coming to stand behind my chair. I could feel his heat radiating against my back. "It sucked."

"You left," Mercer said. "You walked out. You took the quiet with you."

He reached out. His hand trembled—just a fraction—before his fingers brushed my cheek.

"And the noise came back," Mercer confessed. "Louder. Violent."

He looked at Kevin then. Just a glance. A dismissal.

"Move," Mercer said.

Kevin didn't pack his bag. He didn't argue. He scrambled up, grabbing his laptop, and bolted toward the stairs.

Mercer looked back at me.

"Come home," he said.

It wasn't a question. It was a plea wrapped in an order.

"I can't be a pet," I said, though my resolve was melting like wax under a blowtorch. "I need to breathe."

"Then breathe us," Rook said. He dropped to his knees right there on the library floor.

The gasp from the watching students was audible. The Enforcer. The monster. Kneeling in public.

Rook rested his forehead against my arm. "We won't lock you in. You can go to class. You can keep your little lab coat. You can dissect frogs. We don't care."

"Just come back to the bed at night," Mercer said. "Just let us hold you when the lights go out."

"Negotiation," I said, a watery smile touching my lips. "The Captain is negotiating?"

"I am surrendering," Mercer corrected.

He held out his hand. Palm up. A massive, calloused invitation.

"We are incomplete," Mercer said. "The data is conclusive. We don't function without the third element."

I looked at his hand. I looked at Rook, kneeling beside me, pressing his face into the fabric of the hoodie I hadn't taken off.

They were crazy. They were possessive. They were overwhelming.

But they were mine.

I closed my textbook. The sound was final.

I placed my hand in Mercer's. His fingers crushed down instantly, interlocking, sealing the pact.

"Take me home," I said.

Mercer hauled me up. He pulled me into his chest, burying his face in my hair, inhaling like a drowning man breaking the surface.

"Home," he agreed.

Rook stood up, wrapping his arms around both of us from behind, creating the fortress again.

"And we're burning the library," Rook muttered into my ear. "Or at least that chair. That guy smelled like vanilla. I hate vanilla."

"Let's just go," I laughed, a broken, happy sound.

They walked me out. Flanked on both sides. Shielded. Claimed.

I caught a glimpse of myself in the glass doors as we left. I looked small between them. Helpless, almost.

But then I saw their faces. The relief. The devotion. The way they oriented their massive bodies around mine to block the wind.

I wasn't the pet.

I was the leash.

Chapter Seventeen

A Violent Sobriety

POV: Mina

My dorm room was a coffin.

Twelve by twelve feet of cinder block walls painted a tenant-grade beige. A twin mattress that felt like a slab of concrete compared to the cloud I had slept on the night before. The air was stale, smelling of old textbooks and lemon pledge, sterile and thin.

I curled on my side, knees drawn to my chest.

My body was going into shock.

It wasn't a metaphor. My skin felt tight, feverish, the nerve endings raw and screaming for contact that wasn't there. I rubbed my cheek against the coarse pillowcase, but it didn't smell like sandalwood. It didn't smell like ozone or the dark, heavy musk of an alpha male in rut. It smelled like laundry detergent and loneliness.

Eight hours.

I had been gone for eight hours.

Logic stated I should be relieved. I had escaped the event horizon of a black hole. Mercer and Rook were consuming me, erasing the boundaries of my identity until I was nothing but a support system for their dysfunction. I had walked out to save myself. To preserve Mina the Student, Mina the Scientist.

But Mina the Scientist was currently analyzing the data, and the results were catastrophic.

My heart rate wouldn't settle. A dull, throbbing ache pulsed low in my stomach, a phantom reminder of how full I had been. My thighs still bore the faint, darkening impressions of Mercer's grip, and every time the fabric of my sweatpants brushed against them, I flinched, expecting a hand that wasn't there.

I sat up. The room spun.

"Focus," I whispered. My voice sounded thin, reedy.

I dragged myself to the wobbly wooden desk. My laptop sat open, the screen glowing with a half-finished lab report on cellular respiration. *ATP production. Energy transfer.*

I stared at the words. They swam.

Usually, the structure of biology soothed me. The predictable rules of life. Cells divide. Mitochondria power the system. Organisms adapt or die.

But my biology had been hacked.

I wasn't adapting. I was dying.

I typed a sentence. Deleted it. The silence in the room was deafening. I missed the heavy, rhythmic thud of Rook's boots. I missed the terrifying stillness of Mercer watching me from a doorway. I missed the constant, suffocating weight of their attention.

My phone buzzed on the desk.

I snatched it up, my pulse spiking.

No text. No call. Just a notification from the campus sports app.

BREAKING: Practice Brawl Suspends Captain and Enforcer.

My stomach dropped.

I tapped the notification. A video loaded. It was shaky footage, clearly filmed by a fan in the stands of the practice arena.

The ice was a sheet of white glare. The players were blurs of movement. And then, in the center circle, chaos.

Two giants.

Mercer had abandoned his stick. He had Rook by the cage of his helmet, shaking him violently. Rook wasn't backing down. He threw a punch—a gloved, heavy blow that connected with the side of Mercer's helmet with a crack that the microphone picked up even over the shouting.

They weren't sparring. They weren't posturing.

They were trying to kill each other.

The rest of the team scrambled to separate them. Three guys grabbed Rook, hauling him back by his jersey. It took two more to restrain Mercer.

I brought the phone closer, my eyes scanning the pixels.

Mercer didn't look angry. He looked rabid. His helmet had been knocked askew, revealing a face twisted into a snarl of pure, unadulterated misery.

Rook was shouting something, spitting the words out with blood and saliva. I turned the volume up, pressing the speaker to my ear.

...where is she?

The audio was distorted, but the cadence was unmistakable.

You let her go! You let her walk out!

My hand shook. The phone clattered onto the desk.

They were tearing each other apart because the buffer was gone. I was the chemical agent that kept the mixture stable, and without me, the reaction was volatile.

I should be terrified. These were violent men. Men who solved problems with their fists and their weight. Men who viewed the world as something to be conquered or destroyed.

But I wasn't terrified.

A warm, wet heat pooled between my legs.

I wanted them to fight. I wanted them to bleed. I wanted to be the only thing soft enough to staunch the wound.

"Stupid," I hissed, digging my fingernails into my palms. "You are not a bandage."

I stood up, pacing the small length of the room. Three steps, turn. Three steps, turn. A caged animal.

I needed to go somewhere. Anywhere. This room was shrinking. The walls were closing in, pressing against my ribs.

I grabbed my bag. I shoved the laptop inside, not bothering to close the document. I needed neutral ground. The library. The one place on campus where silence was enforced, where I could hide behind stacks of books and pretend I wasn't a woman unraveling at the seams.

I pulled on a generic grey sweatshirt. It was too small. The cuffs rode up my wrists. It felt flimsy, like paper.

I hesitated.

My hand drifted to the pile of clothes on the floor. Mercer's charcoal hoodie lay there, a dark puddle of fabric.

I shouldn't. It was a symbol of ownership. Wearing it was a capitulation.

I grabbed it.

I stripped off the grey sweatshirt and pulled the charcoal one over my head.

The scent hit me instantly. Cedar. Sweat. The sharp, metallic tang of the Captain. It coated my senses, filling my lungs with a heavy, drug-like calm. My shoulders dropped two inches. The frantic buzzing in my brain quieted to a dull hum.

The fabric swallowed me, hanging to my mid-thighs. It was armor. It was a claim.

I walked out of the dorm.

The hallway was busy. Students moved past, laughing, complaining about exams, existing in a world of normal, low-stakes problems. They looked at me—the small girl in the massive hoodie—and looked away. They didn't see the mark on me. They didn't see that I belonged to the monsters on the news feed.

I kept my head down.

Outside, the air was crisp, biting with the promise of autumn. I walked fast, hugging my books to my chest.

"Mina?"

I froze.

Kevin stood near the bike racks. He held a helmet in one hand, looking wholesome and safe and completely irrelevant.

"Hey," he said, jogging over. "I haven't seen you in class. You missed the lecture on enzymatic reactions."

"I was sick," I lied. My voice sounded rusty, unused.

"You look..." He paused, his eyes scanning my face. "Tired. Are you okay?"

I looked at him. He was nice. He was safe. If I dated Kevin, we would go to movies. We would hold hands. We would have sex in the dark, under the covers, and he would ask if I was okay every time he moved.

The thought made my skin crawl.

"I'm fine," I said. "Just stress."

"Do you want to study?" Kevin asked, gesturing toward the library. "I'm heading there now. I have a spot in the back. It's quiet."

Quiet.

Rook wasn't quiet. Rook was a hurricane. He laughed loud, he groaned loud, he fucked loud.

"Sure," I heard myself say. "Study."

Maybe if I sat next to normal, the abnormal cravings would fade. Maybe exposure to a standard male baseline would reset my sensors.

We walked to the library. Kevin talked about his engineering project. Bridges. Load-bearing structures.

"The key is tension," Kevin explained as we pushed through the glass doors. "Too much tension, it snaps. Too little, it sags. You have to find the equilibrium."

I stopped in the lobby.

Equilibrium.

Mercer and Rook didn't have equilibrium. They had torque. They had force. And I wasn't the tension that snapped; I was the suspension cable holding the whole damn bridge together.

"Mina?" Kevin held the inner door open.

I followed him in. The library was cool, smelling of old paper and dust. We found a table in the back corner, secluded by rows of bound periodicals.

I sat down. I opened my book. *Cellular Mitosis.*

I read the same paragraph four times.

Prophase. Metaphase. Anaphase. Separation.

My phone buzzed again.

I shouldn't look.

I looked.

A text from an unknown number. No name. Just a message.

We're bleeding.

Two words.

My breath hitched. It was Rook. It had to be. Mercer wouldn't text. Mercer would drive a tank through the wall.

I stared at the screen. The letters blurred.

We're bleeding.

Not 'I'm bleeding.' *We.* They were a single organism again, injured and lashing out.

"Bad news?" Kevin whispered.

I looked up. "What?"

"You look like you saw a ghost," he said. He reached across the table, his hand brushing mine. His skin was dry. Warm. Human.

I yanked my hand back.

The reaction was instinctual. A violent rejection of unauthorized touch.

Kevin blinked, hurt flashing in his eyes. "Woah. Sorry. I just..."

"Don't," I snapped.

Then I felt it.

A shift in the air pressure. A drop in the temperature. The fine hairs on the back of my neck stood up, electrified.

The library was silent, but the quality of the silence had changed. It wasn't the hush of study anymore. It was the hush of a forest when a predator enters the clearing.

I smelled them before I saw them.

The scent cut through the dust and old paper. Sandalwood. Ice. The metallic bite of fresh violence.

My heart slammed against my ribs, a trapped bird realizing the cage door was open.

I turned my head.

They stood at the end of the aisle.

They looked wrecked.

Mercer's lip was split. A dark bruise blossomed along his jawline, purple and angry against his pale skin. He wasn't wearing a suit. He wore black jeans and a black t-shirt that clung to his chest, damp with sweat. He looked like he had run here. Or fought his way here.

Rook stood just behind him. His eye was swollen shut. There was dried blood on his chin. His knuckles were wrapped in hasty, unraveling tape.

They weren't looking at the books. They weren't looking at the other students.

They were looking at Kevin.

And the look wasn't human. It was cold, flat, and terrifyingly devoid of mercy.

Kevin followed my gaze. He turned in his chair.

"Holy shit," he breathed.

Mercer took a step forward. His boots made no sound on the carpet, but the movement felt heavy, like the displacement of water by a shark.

He ignored Kevin. His blue eyes—darker now, almost navy with adrenaline—shifted to me. He took in the hoodie. He took in the way my hands were clutching the edge of the table.

He didn't smile.

"Found her," Mercer said. His voice was a low rasp, rough like gravel.

"She's wearing the colors," Rook noted. He stepped out from behind Mercer. He looked unstable. Vibrating with energy. "She didn't take it off."

"Mina?" Kevin's voice wobbled. "Do you know these guys?"

I stood up. My legs felt weak, watery.

"Yes," I whispered.

Mercer didn't stop until his thighs hit the edge of the table. He leaned over, placing his palms flat on the wood. The wood groaned under the pressure.

He looked at Kevin. Just for a second.

"Leave," Mercer said.

It wasn't a request. It was an eviction notice.

Kevin looked at Mercer, then at Rook, whose good eye was fixed on Kevin's throat with alarming intensity. Kevin was an engineer. He understood load-bearing limits. He understood when a structure was about to collapse on his head.

He grabbed his bag. "I'm going. I'm gone."

He scrambled away, abandoning his dignity in the aisle.

I was alone with them.

The silence stretched, thin and tight.

"You fought," I said. I reached out, my fingers hovering over the bruise on Mercer's jaw.

Mercer leaned into my hand. He closed his eyes, a shudder running through his massive frame. He turned his face, pressing a kiss to my palm. His lips were hot. Feverish.

"We broke," Mercer corrected. He opened his eyes. They were wrecked. "The system failed. We tried to reset it, but the inputs were wrong."

"You hurt him," I said, looking at Rook.

Rook stepped closer. He dropped to his knees right there on the library carpet, ignoring the gasps from the few students brave enough to watch. He wrapped his arms around my waist, pressing his face into the hoodie.

"He hurt me because I wanted to burn the city down to find you," Rook mumbled into my stomach. "He told me to wait. I didn't want to wait."

"We waited," Mercer said. He walked around the table. He stood behind me. I was sandwiched between them again. The heavy wall of Mercer at my back, the desperate grip of Rook at my front.

My withdrawal symptoms vanished.

The ache in my stomach settled into a warm, heavy hum. The buzzing in my brain went quiet. The puzzle pieces clicked back into place.

"You're bleeding," I said softly, my hand threading through Rook's sweaty hair.

"We heal," Mercer said. His hand came up to grip the back of my neck, his thumb finding the pulse point. "If the anchor holds."

"I'm not a stress toy," I said, repeating my defense from the morning, though it lacked heat now.

"No," Mercer agreed. He lowered his head until his mouth was at my ear. "Toys are replaceable. You are the structural integrity of the unit."

Rook looked up. His one good eye was wet.

"Come home, mouse," he pleaded. "We bought you a microscope. We bought you the whole damn science department if you want it. Just don't make us sleep in the quiet again."

I looked down at him. The monster on his knees.

I looked at the textbooks on the table. The life I was supposed to want. Safe. Predictable. lonely.

Then I looked at the blood on Rook's cheek. The bruise on Mercer's face. The damage they had inflicted on themselves because they didn't know how to exist without my softness to absorb the impact.

They were broken. They were dangerous.

And they were mine.

"Okay," I whispered.

Rook let out a sound that was half-sob, half-laugh. He buried his face deeper into my stomach.

Mercer's grip on my neck tightened. Possessive. Final.

"Good," Mercer said. "Now let's go. Rook is right. That boy smelled like vanilla. And I have a sudden, violent need to smell nothing but you."

Chapter Eighteen

PREY DRIVE

POV: Mercer

The elevator ride up to the penthouse was silent, but it was the kind of silence that screamed.

I watched the numbers climb—34, 35, 36—and fought the urge to shatter the display panel with my fist. My blood was running too hot, a frantic, chemical burn under my skin that hadn't settled since I saw that vanilla-scented civilian sitting next to her.

Mina stood between us.

She was so small. That was the data point my brain kept tripping over. Five feet of soft, inefficient biology wrapped in my hoodie. A stiff wind could knock her over. And yet, she was the only reason Rook wasn't currently in a holding cell for manslaughter, and the only reason I wasn't tearing the leather interior of the elevator to shreds.

Rook was vibrating. I could feel the tremors radiating off him, a low-frequency hum of pure instability. He was staring at the back of her head, his hands twitching at his sides, fighting the muscle memory of the brawl we'd just left on the ice.

The doors slid open.

The penthouse was exactly as we left it: a wreck. Furniture overturned. Glass on the floor. A monument to our loss of control.

Mina stepped out first. She hesitated, looking at the chaos.

"We made a mess," she whispered.

"We were looking for something," I said. My voice sounded wrecked, unfamiliar to my own ears.

Rook didn't wait. The moment the elevator doors sealed behind us, the leash snapped.

"Prey," Rook growled.

It wasn't a word; it was a classification.

Mina spun around, but Rook was already moving. He didn't walk; he launched. He closed the distance in two strides, grabbing her by the waist and hauling her off her feet.

She gasped, a sharp intake of air that hit my ears like a starter pistol.

"Rook," I warned, though I didn't move to stop him.

"No," Rook snarled, backing her into the nearest wall. He pinned her there with his body, his forearm bracketing her head, his hips grinding against hers. "She smelled like paper. She smelled like dust. I need to fix it."

Mina didn't scream. She didn't struggle. She looked up at him, her eyes wide, realizing the danger she had invited back into her life. We weren't the civilized captains of industry right now. We were animals who had been starved for eight hours.

I walked toward them.

I needed to touch her. My hands ached with it. A phantom pain.

"Put her down," I ordered, though the command lacked conviction.

"Make me," Rook challenged, burying his face in her neck, inhaling violently. "She's ours, Merc. Tell me she's ours."

Mina looked at me over Rook's massive shoulder. Her gaze didn't hold fear. It held a dark, heavy recognition. She saw the monster. She saw the break in the armor.

And she liked it.

"I'm yours," she said. Her voice was steady, cutting through the red haze in my brain. "But if you bruise me where it shows, I can't wear the low-cut dress to the gala next week."

The mundane practicality of the statement acted like a bucket of ice water.

Rook froze. He pulled back an inch, blinking, his chest heaving like a bellows.

"Gala?" Rook blinked.

"The Foundation dinner," Mina said, reaching up to touch the split in his lip. "You have to wear tuxes. I have to look pretty. Bruises aren't pretty."

She was managing us. Even pinned against a wall, feet dangling off the floor, she was calibrating the threat level.

I stepped into her space. I occupied the air behind Rook, boxing her in completely.

"We aren't going to the gala," I said, reaching out to trace the line of her jaw. My thumb rested on her pulse. It hammered against my skin, a frantic, bird-like rhythm that betrayed her calm facade. "We aren't leaving this apartment for a week. We are going to lock the doors, order protein, and remind you why you don't walk away from the unit."

"Is that a threat, Captain?" she asked.

"It is a biological imperative," I corrected.

Mina's eyes dropped. She stopped looking at my face and looked at my chest. She reached out, her small hands grabbing the hem of my black t-shirt.

"Take it off," she ordered.

I went still. "Excuse me?"

"Take it off," she repeated, her voice dropping an octave, thick with a sudden, localized thirst. "I want to see the damage."

I looked at Rook. He was watching us, his pupils blown so wide his eyes looked entirely black. He slowly lowered Mina to the floor but kept his hands on her hips, anchoring her.

I grabbed the hem of my shirt and ripped it over my head.

The fabric tore—a seam popping at the shoulder—but I didn't care. I threw it onto the pile of broken glass and stood bare-chested under the recessed lighting.

Mina inhaled sharply.

She didn't look away. She stepped out of Rook's grip and walked the single step to me. She didn't touch me immediately. She just looked.

Her gaze felt physical. It traced the heavy slope of my traps, the thick cords of muscle in my neck, the scars mapping my ribs from years of taking pucks and sticks for the team. She looked at my arms, analyzing the veins that roped over the biceps, swollen with adrenaline.

"It's unfair," she murmured, her eyes dark and heavy. "To hide all this under a suit. It's like keeping a panther in a cardboard box."

She reached out, her fingers skimming the hard slab of my pectoral muscle. Her touch was cool, a shocking contrast to the fever heat of my skin.

"Look at you," she whispered, her gaze dropping lower, to the V-line disappearing into my jeans. "You're so... dense. heavy. Just acres of mean, hard muscle designed to hurt people."

She looked up, and her pupils were dilated, mirroring ours.

"And you want to use all that on me," she said. It wasn't a question. It was a marvel. "You want to take this body—this weapon that scares grown men—and press it into me until I can't remember my own name."

My control snapped.

The logic center of my brain, the part that calculated angles and PR risks, went dark. There was only the need. The absolute, suffocating need to be inside the exception.

"Not just me," I rasped, grabbing her hand and pressing it flat against the center of my chest so she could feel the violent kick of my heart. "Him too."

I nodded at Rook.

Rook didn't need further invitation. He stripped his own shirt off in a frantic blur of motion.

"Bedroom," I commanded.

"Floor," Rook countered. "Now."

He was right. We wouldn't make the bedroom.

I grabbed Mina by the back of the hoodie—my hoodie—and pulled her flush against me. I bent down, crushing my mouth to hers.

It wasn't a kiss. It was a raid.

I plundered her mouth, tasting the coffee she'd had earlier, tasting her breath, tasting the submissive little noise she made in the back of her throat. I bit her lip, hard enough to sting, punishing her for the library, for the vanilla boy, for the eight hours of silence.

Rook was on her instantly. He dropped to his knees behind her, his hands gripping her thighs, dragging her leggings down with a ruthlessness that ripped the fabric.

"Mine," Rook mumbled against the skin of her ass. "Perfect. Soft."

Mina gasped into my mouth as Rook's stubble grazed her hip. She clung to my shoulders, her nails digging into the skin, anchoring herself as we dismantled her defenses.

"Wait," she panted, breaking the kiss. "The prep—"

"No prep," I growled, lifting her up. "You're already wet. I can smell it."

I walked her backward until her legs hit the edge of the sprawling oak dining table. I swept the expensive vase and the mail onto the floor with a crash. I lifted her onto the wood.

She scrambled back, looking between us. Two giants. Two monsters.

"You can't fit," she whispered, looking at the bulge in my jeans, then at Rook's. "Not both. Not like this."

"We fit," Rook said, standing up. He shoved his jeans down, freeing himself. He was heavy, thick, and fully hard. "We always fit. You stretch."

He moved behind her on the table, spreading her legs wide, stepping between them. He didn't hesitate. He lined himself up and pushed.

Mina cried out—a high, sharp sound that tore through the room.

Rook groaned, his head falling back, the cords in his neck straining. He didn't stop. He drove into her, inch by inch, stretching her tight, filling the space that had been empty for too long.

"God," Rook hissed. "So tight. You tried to close up on us."

"I didn't," she sobbed, her hands scrabbling on the table.

"Liar," I said.

I stepped between her drawn-up knees. Rook was buried deep inside her, his hips snapping forward with a desperate, jerky rhythm. His hands were on her waist, holding her in place for his use.

But her mouth was empty. Her eyes were searching.

I unbuckled my belt.

Mina watched. She watched the leather slide through the loops. She watched me free myself. She didn't look scared anymore. She looked hungry. She looked like a devotee waiting for the idol to fall.

"Please," she whimpered.

The word shattered me.

I leaned over her, bracing my hands on the table on either side of her head. I boxed her in. Rook below, owning her body. Me above, owning her breath.

"Open," I ordered.

She opened her mouth.

I didn't kiss her. I pushed past her lips, feeding her my thumb first, pressing down on her tongue, making her taste me. She sucked on it, her eyes rolling back, her body bowing off the table as Rook hit a sensitive spot deep inside her.

"Good girl," I praised, my voice dark and thick. "Take it all."

I replaced my thumb with myself.

I didn't thrust. I just held her there, impaled on both ends, filled completely by the team.

The sensation was blinding. The heat of her mouth, the wet suction, combined with the visual of Rook claiming her from below—it was a sensory overload that threatened to end me in seconds.

I forced myself to look at her.

Tears were streaming down her face. Her mascara was smeared. Her hair was a chaotic halo around her head. She looked wrecked. She looked ruined.

She looked perfect.

"Say it," I demanded, pulling back just enough to let her speak. "Say you aren't leaving."

"I can't," she choked out, her hips bucking to meet Rook's thrusts. "I'm... stuck."

"Damn right you're stuck," Rook growled, leaning forward to bite the curve of her shoulder. "We're welding the doors shut."

I slammed back into her mouth.

The pace picked up. It wasn't lovemaking. It was a frantic, sweaty exorcism of the day's fear. Rook was pounding into her, his grunts low and animalistic. I was using her mouth with a rhythm that matched his, a perfect, synchronized assault.

We were a unit. A tripod. Without her, we were just two violent men beating the hell out of each other. With her, we were a system.

Mina's hand came up, finding my hair, gripping tight. She wasn't pushing me away. She was pulling me closer.

"Mercer," she tried to say around me.

I pulled out, gasping, needing air.

"I'm here," I said, dropping my forehead to hers.

"Don't stop," she begged. "Don't you dare stop."

"Never," I promised.

I grabbed her leg, hooking it over my shoulder, exposing her completely to my view. I watched Rook disappear inside her, watched her body stretch and accommodate the impossible size of him. It was a miracle of biology. A soft, yielding miracle that somehow managed to contain us.

I looked at Rook. He found my gaze.

The aggression in his eyes was gone, replaced by a glazed, euphoric peace.

"She fits," Rook whispered, sweat dripping from his nose onto her stomach.

"She fits," I agreed.

I grabbed Mina's face, forcing her to look at me.

"You are the buffer," I told her, the truth of it hitting me harder than any check into the boards. "You are the quiet. And if you ever try to walk out of a library again, I will burn the entire campus to the ground to drag you back."

Mina smiled. It was a broken, beautiful thing.

"Okay," she whispered. "Burn it."

I kissed her, swallowing her sob, and let the darkness take us.

Chapter Nineteen

Wrecked by Softness

POV: Mina

The mattress dipped.

It wasn't a gentle motion. It was the sudden, seismic shift of nearly five hundred pounds of erratic male aggression collapsing onto the bed.

I scrambled backward on the sheets, my back hitting the padded headboard. The room was dark, lit only by the city spill coming through the floor-to-ceiling windows, casting long, fractured shadows across the duvet. My heart slammed a frantic rhythm against my ribs—*thump-thump-thump*—patterning the silence with the noise of my own survival instinct.

Mercer stood at the foot of the bed. He was terrifying.

His chest heaved. The bruises from the practice brawl were already darkening on his ribs, painting violent abstract art across his pale skin. He looked at me not like a lover, but like a starving man staring at the last loaf of bread in a famine.

Rook was already on the bed. He crawled toward me on his hands and knees, a predator stalking across the high-thread-count plains. The split in his lip oozed a fresh drop of blood. He didn't wipe it away.

"You smell like him," Rook rasped. He stopped inches from my knees, sniffing the air near my skin. "Vanilla. Paper. Bland."

"I don't," I whispered. My voice broke. "I smell like you. Look at me. I'm wearing your clothes. I'm in your bed."

"Not enough," Mercer said.

He moved. He didn't walk; he stormed. He climbed onto the mattress, his weight settling on my other side, effectively boxing me in. Six-foot-six of ice and six-foot-six of fire, and me, the fragile biology experiment in the middle.

Mercer reached out. His hand wrapped around my ankle. His grip wasn't painful, but it was absolute. An iron shackle. He dragged me down the bed until I lay flat, staring up at the ceiling.

"We need to Scrub it off," Mercer stated. He loomed over me, bracing his hands on either side of my head. Sweat dripped from his nose, landing on my cheek. It was hot. Salty. "We need to put the mark back on."

"Mercer, you're bleeding," I said, reaching up to touch the cut on his cheekbone.

He caught my wrist. He turned his face into my palm, biting the fleshy part of my thumb. Hard.

"Pain is data," he mumbled against my skin. "This? You leaving? That was system failure. That was a crash."

Rook made a low, wounded noise in his throat. He shifted, settling his heavy hips between my spread legs. He didn't ask. He didn't prep. He assumed the position of ownership because, in his mind, the deed was already signed in blood.

"Open," Rook demanded.

I obeyed. My legs fell apart, heavy and useless.

Rook didn't enter me yet. He just pressed the head of his cock against me, hot and wet and impossibly large. He ground down, friction sparking along my nerves. He watched my face, looking for fear, looking for rejection.

He found neither.

I arched my back. A wet sound echoed in the quiet room.

"Please," I begged.

"Please what?" Mercer asked. He lowered his body until his chest crushed my breasts, his weight pressing the air from my lungs. It should have been suffocating. It felt like a weighted blanket, grounding me to the earth.

"Please fix it," I sobbed. "Make it quiet again."

Mercer kissed me. It wasn't sweet. It was a collision. He devoured my mouth, his tongue sweeping through, tasting the panic and the desire. At the same moment, Rook pushed forward.

He didn't snap his hips. He sank into me slowly, stretching me, filling the void that had ached for eight hours. He was too big. He was always too big. But my body remembered him. My muscles yielded, wrapping around the invasion, welcoming the monster home.

"God," Rook groaned, his forehead dropping to rest on my stomach. "Home. She's home."

"Look at her," Mercer ordered, breaking the kiss but keeping his face inches from mine. "Watch her take it."

Rook lifted his head. His dark eyes were glassy, drugged with endorphins. He watched the way my body stretched to accommodate him. He watched a tear slide from the corner of my eye into my hair.

"Does it hurt?" Rook asked, voice rough.

"Yes," I gasped.

"Good," Mercer growled. He bit my neck, right over the pulse point. "Remember it. Next time you think about walking out a door, remember how this feels. You don't fit out there, Mina. You're ruined for them. You're too wide for small men."

It was a cruel thing to say. It was the truest thing I had ever heard.

I wrapped my legs around Rook's waist, pulling him deeper. "I know. I know."

Rook began to move. Long, punishing strokes. He wasn't fucking me for pleasure; he was fucking me for reassurance. Every thrust was a question: *Are you here?* Every clench of my body was the answer: *Yes.*

Mercer refused to be left out. He needed contact. He ran his large hands down my sides, counting my ribs, his fingers digging into the soft flesh of my hips.

"You're so small," Mercer marveled, his voice dipping into a dangerous frequency. "Fragile. Breakable. But you hold us. How do you hold us?"

"I don't know," I cried out as Rook hit a spot deep inside that made my vision blur.

"Inefficient," Mercer decided. "But necessary."

He moved his hand between our bodies. He found me. He didn't use finesse. He used the same relentless pressure he used on the ice. His thumb circled the bundle of nerves already screaming for release, adding a sharp, electric spike to the heavy thud of Rook's rhythm.

I shattered.

It wasn't a graceful peak. It was a frantic, clawing unraveling. I screamed, my head thrashing on the pillow. My fingernails dug into Mercer's shoulders, likely drawing blood to match the bruises.

Rook roared, a guttural sound of triumph. He sped up, chasing me into the dark. He pounded into me—hard, fast, desperate—until he stiffened, his massive body bowing like a drawn bowstring. He poured himself into me, shaking with the force of it, groaning my name like it was a prayer.

Mercer didn't stop. He kept touching me, kept kissing me, kept demanding my attention even as my body went boneless.

"Don't sleep," Mercer commanded. "Stay."

Rook collapsed. He fell forward, his weight crushing me into the mattress. He buried his face in the crook of my neck, his breathing ragid and wet.

"Don't move," Rook mumbled into my skin. "Don't you dare move."

"I can't," I wheezed. "You're squishing me."

"Good."

Mercer rolled off me, but only far enough to lie on my other side. He pulled the duvet up, covering the three of us in a cocoon of heat and musk.

The silence returned.

But it wasn't the empty, howling silence of the dorm room. This silence had weight. It had texture. It was filled with the sound of three hearts slowing down, trying to find a synchronized beat.

I lay there, sandwiched between the walls of muscle. My body throbbed. I felt stretched, used, and impossibly full.

Mercer propped himself up on one elbow. He looked down at me. His blue eyes were clear now. The red haze of the fight was gone, replaced by a clinical, possessive focus.

He reached out and brushed a damp strand of hair off my forehead.

"The vanilla boy," Mercer said quietly. "Did he touch you?"

I shook my head. "He shook my hand. That's all."

"Hand," Mercer repeated. He grabbed my right hand—the one Kevin had touched. He brought it to his lips. He licked the palm, slow and deliberate, erasing the memory of the handshake. Then he bit the pad of my thumb, hard enough to leave a mark.

"Sanitized," Mercer declared.

Rook lifted his head. He looked like a wreck. His eye was swelling shut, turning a nasty shade of purple.

"My turn," Rook said.

He grabbed my hand from Mercer and pressed it to his own battered face. He rubbed his cheek against my palm like a cat, smearing a trace of blood on my skin.

"You like the blood," Rook accused softly. "I saw you in the library. You liked it."

"I hated it," I lied.

"Liar." Rook grinned, a crooked, painful expression. "You got wet. I could smell it from the door. You like knowing we bleed for you."

I looked at the ceiling. "It makes me feel... valuable."

"Valuable?" Mercer scoffed. He dropped back onto the pillow, draping an arm heavily across my waist. "Value implies a market price. There is no market. You are a singularity."

"A what?"

"A black hole," Mercer clarified. "You suck all the light out of the room, and all we can do is orbit you until we get pulled in and crushed."

It was the most romantic, terrifying thing anyone had ever said to me.

"I'm not going to crush you," I whispered.

"You already did," Rook murmured, his eyes closing. "We were doing fine, mouse. We were cold. We were perfect. Then you showed up with your kittens and your sweaters and your big, sad eyes. Now look at us. Brawling in practice. Stalking students."

"Pathetic," Mercer agreed. He didn't sound angry. He sounded resigned.

I turned on my side, facing Rook. I traced the line of his jaw.

"I tried to leave," I said. "For you. To give you your game back."

Rook's eye snapped open. "Don't."

"I thought—"

"Don't think," Mercer interrupted from behind me. He pulled me back against his chest, spooning me so tightly I could feel the slow, heavy beat of his heart against my spine. "We do the thinking. You do the existing."

"That sounds like a dictatorship," I muttered.

"It is," Mercer said. "But it comes with a private lab and unconditional worship. The benefits package is competitive."

I laughed. It was a small, tired sound, but it broke the last of the tension.

Rook shifted, wincing as his bruises protested. He draped his arm over me, his hand clasping Mercer's hand where it rested on my stomach. They linked fingers, locking me in a cage of flesh and bone.

"We have a problem though," Rook said, his voice slurring with sleep.

"What?" I asked.

"Suspended," Rook yawned. "Coach is gonna be pissed. No game on Saturday."

"We'll pay the fine," Mercer dismissed. "We have the weekend off. We can run tests."

"Tests?" I felt a spike of wariness.

"Endurance tests," Mercer mumbled into my hair. "Range of motion. Sensory deprivation. We need to calibrate the new equipment."

"I'm the equipment, aren't I?"

"Obviously."

I closed my eyes. The heat was overwhelming. The smell of them—cedar, ozone, sex—filled my lungs, engaging the receptors that had been screaming in the dorm room.

I was a scientist. I understood variables. I understood cause and effect.

The effect of leaving them was chaos. The effect of staying was this: being crushed, overwhelmed, and completely stripped of autonomy.

But as Mercer's breathing evened out and Rook's thumb stroked the skin of my hip in a rhythmic, unconscious comfort, I realized the data was flawed.

I wasn't the victim here.

They were the ones who had broken protocol. They were the ones who had shattered their own rules to drag me back. They were the ones who were terrified of the quiet.

I snuggled deeper into the mattress, pulling their arms tighter around me.

"Okay," I whispered to the dark. "Run the tests."

Mercer squeezed my waist. Rook let out a long, contented sigh.

The cage locked. And for the first time in eight hours, I finally fell asleep.

Chapter Twenty

STANDARD DEVIATION

POV: Mina

The morning light was an intruder. It sliced through the gap in the blackout curtains, a sharp blade of white cutting across the chaotic landscape of the bed.

I didn't move. I couldn't have moved if the building caught fire.

Rook lay sprawled across my lower half, a dead weight of scarred muscle and heat. His face was buried in the mattress by my hip, one massive arm thrown over my legs, effectively pinning me to the sheets. He snored—a low, rumbling growl that vibrated through my bones.

Mercer was awake.

I felt his gaze before I saw him. It was a physical pressure, heavier than the duvet, tracking the rise and fall of my chest. He lay on his side, propped up on one elbow, his other hand resting flat on my stomach. His fingers were long, precise, and currently tracing the faint red marks his grip had left on my skin hours ago.

"Bruising," Mercer murmured. His voice was a wreck—gravel grinding against glass. "Subcutaneous hemorrhage. It covers twelve percent of your surface area."

"It doesn't hurt," I whispered. My throat felt raw. Used.

Mercer's blue eyes snapped to mine. They weren't cold today. They were fever-bright, rimmed with red, the pupils blown wide enough to swallow the iris. He looked like a man who had survived a plane crash and was still trying to figure out if he was alive.

"Liar," he rasped. "I was not gentle. Rook was... catastrophic."

"I didn't want gentle."

Mercer's hand moved. He slid his palm up my ribcage, over the curve of my breast, stopping at the hollow of my throat. He felt my pulse. It kicked against his thumb—fast, erratic.

"Data supports that assertion," he said. He lowered his head, sniffing the skin of my neck. "You smell like us. Sweat. Semen. Iron. The vanilla is gone."

"Scrubbed," I agreed.

"Good."

He didn't pull back. Instead, he licked the sensitive skin under my ear. A rough, wet stripe. I gasped, my hips bucking instinctively against Rook's weight.

Rook grumbled in his sleep, his arm tightening around my thighs like a python constriction.

"He won't let go," Mercer noted, his mouth moving to my jawline. "He held you for six hours straight. His REM cycle is disturbed. He wakes up every forty minutes to check if you're still solid matter."

"And you?" I asked, weaving my fingers into Mercer's sweaty, tangled hair. "Did you sleep?"

"No." Mercer bit my chin, a sharp nip that made my toes curl. "I watched. I ran the simulations."

"Simulations?"

"outcomes," he corrected. He shifted, his massive body looming over me, blocking out the intrusive sun. "Scenario A: You leave. Rook destabilizes within forty-eight hours. Career-ending violence. I follow shortly after. Alcoholism. Emotional atrophy. The unit dissolves."

He pressed a kiss to my mouth. Hard. Possessive.

"Scenario B," he breathed against my lips. "We keep you. We lock the doors. We feed you. We fuck you until your brain rewires to accept this cage as a habitat while you finish your degree."

"You make it sound so clinical," I murmured, my hands sliding down his back, feeling the ridges of his spine.

"It is clinical," Mercer growled. "It is survival biology. An organism does not voluntarily reject the thing that keeps it alive."

He pulled back, sitting up on his knees. The duvet fell away, revealing the expanse of his chest. He was beautiful in a terrifying, architectural way. Broad shoulders, tapered waist, skin marked by the violence of his sport and the violence of our night.

He grabbed my ankles and dragged me out from under Rook's arm.

Rook roared awake.

It wasn't a waking up; it was a resurrection. He scrambled up, eyes wild, fists clenching the sheets.

"Gone?" Rook shouted, looking around frantically.

"Here," Mercer commanded, pointing at me. "She is here. Calibrate, Rook."

Rook's wild eyes landed on me. He collapsed back onto his heels, his chest heaving. The bruise on his face from the fight was a dark, angry purple, swelling his eye shut. He looked tragic and dangerous, a monster stitched together with bad intentions and good reflexes.

"You moved her," Rook accused, his voice thick with sleep and aggression.

"I needed access," Mercer said simply.

Mercer spread my legs.

The air in the room changed. It thickened. The morning laziness evaporated, replaced by the sharp, electric scent of arousal.

I lay exposed to them. My body was a map of their ownership. Bite marks on my thighs. Finger-shaped bruises on my hips. I felt swollen, tender, and achingly empty.

Mercer looked between my legs. He didn't touch. He just stared, as if he were trying to solve a complex equation written on my skin.

"Pink," Mercer observed softly. "Swollen. We stretched her too far."

"She took it," Rook defended, crawling forward on the bed. He moved like a wolf, low and prowling. He positioned himself behind Mercer, looking over his shoulder. "She liked it. Tell him, mouse. Tell him you liked being full."

"I liked it," I confessed. The shame should have burned me. Instead, it fueled the fire in my belly. "I liked... fitting."

Mercer made a low noise in his throat. He reached out, his thumbs pressing against my inner thighs, parting me further until the stretch burned in a good way.

"Standard deviation," Mercer muttered. "Statistically, you shouldn't exist. A woman who tolerates the force we exert. Who craves the weight."

He lowered his head.

"Mercer?" I gasped.

"Quiet," he ordered. "I am collecting data."

He didn't use his hands. He used his mouth.

Mercer, the Captain, the ice-cold strategist, buried his face between my legs with a hunger that bordered on religious desperation.

His tongue was broad, confident, and relentless. He didn't tease. He claimed. He licked a long, slow stroke from bottom to top, tasting the aftermath of his own seed and my desire.

My back arched off the mattress. A cry tore from my throat—raw and loud.

"Fuck," Rook groaned.

Rook didn't wait. He couldn't. He grabbed my hand, pulling me up into a sitting position while Mercer stayed buried between my legs. I was folded in half, sandwiched between them.

Rook kissed me. It wasn't a kiss; it was a collision of teeth and tongue. He tasted like morning breath and blood, and I drank it down like vintage wine. One of his hands tangled in my hair, holding my head still for his assault, while the other roamed over my breasts, squeezing, kneading, checking for reality.

"So sweet," Rook mumbled into my mouth. "Tastes like sugar. Tastes like mine."

Below, Mercer was destroying me.

He worked with a rhythm that defied logic. Fast, then slow. Hard pressure, then a feather-light flutter that made my nerves scream. He used his teeth on my clit—just a graze, a threat of pain that spiked the pleasure into something blinding.

"Mercer," I sobbed against Rook's lips. "Please. Too much."

Mercer ignored me. He gripped my hips, his fingers digging into the bruises he'd already made, anchoring me to his mouth. He sucked hard, a vacuum seal, drawing everything I was out of my body and into his.

Rook broke the kiss, resting his forehead against mine. His good eye stared into me, dark and dilated.

"Let him worship," Rook whispered, his voice surprisingly tender for a man who had nearly killed a teammate yesterday. "He needs this. He needs to know you're not just a hole. He needs to know you're the altar."

"I can't," I choked out, my head falling back. "I'm going to—"

"Do it," Rook commanded. "Fall apart. We'll catch you."

He moved his hand down, sliding between our bodies, finding the wet heat where Mercer's mouth was working. Rook's fingers pushed inside me.

I screamed.

The intrusion was perfect. Two fingers, thick and calloused, curling inside me, hitting the spot Mercer was simulating from the outside.

I shattered.

It wasn't a wave; it was a demolition. Muscles clamped down on Rook's fingers. My hips thrashed, seeking more friction. Mercer groaned against me, the vibration traveling straight to my core. He drank my release, swallowing every drop, humming with a dark, satisfied greed.

I went boneless.

If Rook hadn't been holding me, I would have collapsed. He lowered me back to the pillows, brushing the damp hair from my forehead.

Mercer lifted his head. His face was wet. His chin shone with my fluids. He didn't wipe it off. He looked proud. He looked like a king who had just conquered a new nation and found the soil fertile.

"Response confirmed," Mercer said, his voice wrecked. "System functional."

He crawled up the bed, moving over me until his face hovered inches from mine. He kissed me—a slow, slick smear of my own taste.

"You are the third leg," Mercer whispered against my lips.

"We need a better metaphor," I weaked, my eyes fluttering shut.

"No," Mercer insisted gently. He grabbed Rook's hand and placed it on my chest, covering it with his own. "A stool. A structure. Two legs cannot stand, Mina. We tried. For three years, we tried to balance. We just kept falling over. Crashing into each other."

Rook nodded, his chin resting on Mercer's shoulder, looking down at me.

"We hurt each other," Rook admitted quietly. "Too much friction. No soft place to land. Just armor hitting armor."

"We need the third point of contact," Mercer said. "The Stabilizer."

I looked at them. The Golden Couple of the NHL. They were massive, wealthy, and adored by millions. And they were looking at me—a broke biology student in a dorm room hoodie—like I was the only thing standing between them and total collapse.

"I can't be a pet," I whispered, the last shred of my resistance surfacing. "I can't just be something you keep in a cage."

Mercer's expression hardened, but not with anger. With resolve.

"You aren't the pet," he corrected. "You are the keeper. We are the monsters, Mina. We are the violent, unstable elements. You are the containment field."

Rook laughed, a short, sharp bark. "He means you're the boss, mouse. You just don't know it yet."

Rook shifted, positioning himself between my legs again. He was hard. Painfully hard. The morning wasn't over for him.

"But right now," Rook growled, the tenderness vanishing as the predator resurfaced. "The monsters are hungry. And you look delicious."

Mercer moved down, settling at my side, his hand gripping my throat lightly—a reminder of who could crush me, and who chose not to.

"Feed us," Mercer ordered softly.

I looked at the ceiling, at the sunlight trying to illuminate the dark corners of their obsession. I stopped fighting the gravity.

I opened my legs wider.

"Eat," I said.

And they did.

Chapter Twenty-One

KEPT BETWEEN THEM

POV: Mina

The world outside the arena doors was a beast waiting to be fed, and I was the raw meat.

Mercer's hand rested on the nape of my neck. It wasn't a casual touch. It was a clamp, a branding iron wrapped in calloused skin. His fingers tangled in the small hairs at the base of my skull, his thumb pressing a rhythm against my vertebrae that matched the terrifying, heavy thud of his own heart.

To my right, Rook was a wall of heat. He radiated a temperature that defied the arena's industrial air conditioning, a furnace fueled by aggression and the specific, high-octane anxiety of a predator cornered.

"Head down," Mercer instructed. His voice was a low vibration that traveled through his arm and into my spine. "Don't look at the lights."

"I can't breathe," I whispered. The air in the concrete tunnel felt thin, sucked out by the sheer mass of the two men bracketing me.

"You don't need to breathe," Rook rumbled, leaning in so close his shoulder brushed my ear. "We breathe for you. Just walk, mouse."

We moved as a single, grotesque organism. A hydra with three heads, two of them snarling and one of them trying not to pass out.

I stared at the floor. The concrete was scuffed, marked by the blades of skates and the heavy boots of equipment managers. But my peripheral vision was filled with *them*.

And God, looking at them hurt.

Mercer had changed out of his practice gear into the mandatory post-game press suit. It was a cruel joke of tailoring. The charcoal fabric strained across the vast, violent expanse of his back, fighting a losing war against the trapezius muscles that rolled like mountain ranges beneath the wool. His thighs, thick as tree trunks, tested the seams of his trousers with every stride. But it was his hands that dried my mouth. They hung by his sides, large and lethal, the knuckles scarred white, veins roping over the back of them like cords of steel. Those hands snapped hockey sticks like toothpicks. Those hands had held my throat this morning while he worshipped me with a gentleness that made me weep.

He was a weapon sheathed in silk. A masterpiece of testosterone and violence, carved from ice and bad intentions.

And Rook... Rook was the fire that melted him. He wore his suit with disdain, the top button undone, his tie crooked. He was broader than Mercer, denser, a block of granite that moved with a terrifying grace. His jaw was dusted with stubble that burned my skin, and his mouth—currently pressed into a thin, white line—was the only thing that had ever made me speak in tongues.

They were magnificent. They were terrifying. They were the NHL's undisputed kings, the gay icons who had shattered ceilings and broken noses.

And I was the biology major in a thrift-store cardigan who was about to ruin everything.

"They're going to see," I murmured, my feet stumbling.

Mercer caught me. He didn't just steady me; he hauled me up, his grip tightening until it bordered on pain.

"Let them see," Mercer said. The coldness in his tone wasn't directed at me. It was directed at the double doors ahead.

"They think you're..." I couldn't finish the sentence. *They think you only want each other.*

"They think we are binary," Mercer corrected. He stopped, forcing Rook to halt with him. He turned me, his massive body blocking out the harsh fluorescent lights of the tunnel. His blue eyes burned with a feverish intensity. "They think the system is closed. Zero and One. They don't know about the variable."

Rook reached out, his large, rough hand cupping my face. He swiped his thumb over my cheekbone, erasing a smudge of mascara I didn't know was there. The gesture was sickeningly sweet, a devastating contrast to the murder in his eyes.

"You're not the secret anymore, Mina," Rook said softly. "You're the prize."

"Doors," a security guard barked from the end of the hall. "Thirty seconds."

Mercer straightened. He adjusted the collar of my cardigan, smoothing the cheap wool as if it were ermine.

"Stay between us," he ordered. "If they ask you a question, you look at me. If they try to touch you, Rook will remove their arm. Understood?"

"Yes," I squeaked.

"Good girl."

The doors burst open.

The noise hit us like a physical blow. A wall of sound—shouting, camera shutters, the roar of a thousand questions merging into a single, deafening frequency.

Flash. Flash. Flash.

The world dissolved into strobing white light.

I flinched, burying my face in Mercer's sleeve. He didn't pull away. He shifted, angling his body to shield me, turning his broad back to the worst of the glare. Rook moved in front, clearing a path through the throng of reporters who surged against the velvet ropes like zombies at a fence.

"Mercer! Mercer! Is it true?"

"Rook! The photos from the library—"

"Who is she? Is she a relative?"

"Mercer, look this way! Are the rumors about the breakup true?"

The questions were darts, tipped with poison. They wanted blood. They wanted the tragedy of the golden couple splitting up. They couldn't conceive of the reality—that the couple wasn't splitting, but expanding.

We moved toward the waiting black SUV at the curb. It was only fifty feet, but it felt like a mile through a war zone.

A microphone boom dipped too low, nearly clipping the top of my head.

Rook moved so fast he blurred.

He snatched the metal pole out of the air. He didn't just push it away; he torqued his wrist, snapping the mechanism with a loud, dry *crack*. He shoved the broken equipment back at the stunned cameraman.

"Back," Rook snarled. It wasn't a request. It was a guttural command from the bottom of the food chain to the top.

The circle of reporters recoiled. The silence that followed lasted exactly one second before the frenzy doubled.

"Did you see that? He's protecting her!"

"Who is she?"

Mercer guided me forward, his hand never leaving my neck. I felt the tension vibrating in him, a high-voltage hum. He hated this. He hated the disorder. He hated the variables he couldn't control.

But he didn't hate me.

He looked down, ignoring the cameras, ignoring the screaming fans behind the barricades. His gaze was heavy, hooded, and frighteningly focused.

"Almost there," he murmured. "Three steps. Two."

A woman with a press badge lunged over the rope. She shoved a phone into Mercer's face. On the screen, a grainy image.

Us.

The dorm room. Yesterday. Mercer pinned against the doorframe, kissing me while Rook knelt at my feet. It was blurry, taken from down the hall, but it was unmistakable. The raw hunger. The submission. The complete, undeniable possession.

"Captain!" the reporter shrieked. "Does this mean you're straight now? Is the 'Man Advantage' a lie?"

I froze. My blood turned to ice.

The narrative. The beautiful, inspiring narrative of the two gay hockey stars finding love in a hopeless place. I had just torched it. I was the arsonist standing in the ashes of their legacy.

Mercer stopped.

The SUV door was open. Safety was right there. But he stopped.

He looked at the photo. He looked at the reporter. Then, slowly, terrifyingly, he looked at me.

The shame clawed up my throat. I tried to pull away, to shrink, to dissolve into the pavement. "I'm sorry," I mouthed. "I'm so sorry."

Mercer's expression didn't flicker. He reached out and took the phone from the reporter's hand. He held it up, studying the image with a clinical detachment.

"Not straight," Mercer said.

His voice wasn't loud, but it cut through the noise like a scalpel. The immediate vicinity went dead silent.

Mercer handed the phone back to the woman. He turned to me, right there on the sidewalk, in front of God and ESPN and everyone.

He smoothed a flyaway hair from my forehead. His touch was reverent. It was the touch of a man handling a holy relic.

"Still gay," Mercer stated, his voice dropping to that dangerous, gravel-rough register that usually meant I was about to be stripped naked. "We don't like women."

He leaned down, pressing a kiss to the crown of my head.

"We just like *her*."

The reporter gaped. "But... she's a girl. That doesn't make sense."

Rook stepped in. He loomed over the reporter, blocking out the sun. He looked at me, his dark eyes softening into that devastating, puppy-dog devotion that terrified me more than his rage.

"It doesn't have to make sense," Rook rumbled. "It just has to fit."

He grabbed my waist. His hands were huge, encompassing my entire midsection. He lifted me—literally lifted me off the ground—and deposited me into the backseat of the SUV like I was a fragile parcel.

Mercer climbed in after me. Rook followed.

The heavy door slammed shut. The locks engaged with a solid *thunk*.

The silence inside the car was instant and absolute. The tinted windows turned the flashing cameras into distant, mute lightning bugs.

I sat in the middle. Always in the middle.

I was shaking. My hands trembled in my lap. I stared at my knees, waiting for the anger. Waiting for the PR lecture. Waiting for them to realize that the cost of keeping me was too high.

"Heart rate is elevated," Mercer observed from my left. "One hundred and forty beats per minute."

"You told them," I whispered. "You just... told them."

"I clarified the data," Mercer said. He reached over and took my trembling hand. He didn't hold it; he began to massage the palm, his thumb working into the tense muscle with precise, medical pressure. "Ambiguity leads to speculation. Speculation leads to chaos."

"But your image," I choked out. "The community. The fans. They're going to hate you. They're going to say I turned you."

"Let them talk," Rook grunted from my right. He had sprawled out, his long legs taking up most of the floor space. He rested his head back against the leather seat, closing his swollen eye. "I don't care about the fans. I care about the fact that you're shivering."

Rook blindly reached out and dragged a heavy wool blanket from the floor, throwing it over my lap. He tucked the edges in around my thighs with clumsy, aggressive care.

"Warm up," he ordered.

I looked at Mercer. He was watching me with that unnerving, unblinking focus. In the dim light of the car, he looked less like a hockey captain and more like a dragon guarding a hoard of one gold coin.

"Why?" I asked. "Why did you do that?"

Mercer leaned in. The scent of him—sandalwood, sweat, and expensive wool—filled the cabin, displacing the oxygen.

"Because you were scared," he said simply. "And when you are scared, you run. I am removing the exit routes."

"You outed us to keep me trapped?"

"I claimed you to keep you safe," Mercer corrected. His hand moved from my palm to my wrist, his fingers circling the bone, sensing the pulse. "We are a closed system, Mina. The world outside doesn't get a vote. But they needed to know the boundaries."

He brought my wrist to his mouth. He kissed the soft, blue-veined skin of my inner arm.

"She is necessary," he murmured against my skin.

The words defied the clinical tone. They were a confession. A surrender.

My chest ached. It was a physical pain, a cracking of the ribs to make room for the enormity of what they were offering. They had just burned down their public identity to build a fortress around me.

Rook opened his good eye. He looked at Mercer, then at me.

"Are they following us?" Rook asked the driver.

"Yes, sir," the driver replied from the front. "Three news vans."

"Good," Rook grunted. He reached under the blanket, his hand finding my knee. He gave it a squeeze that bordered on bruising. "Let 'em follow. Let 'em see where we sleep. Maybe then they'll understand."

"Understand what?" I whispered.

Rook looked at me, a dark, possessive heat flaring in his gaze.

"That we don't share."

Mercer hummed in agreement. He pulled me closer, until my head rested on his shoulder. The stiff wool of his suit scratched my cheek, but beneath it, I could feel the solid, unyielding warmth of him.

"Close your eyes," Mercer commanded softly. "We have a forty-minute drive. I want your heart rate under eighty by the time we get home."

"And if it's not?"

Mercer's lips brushed my forehead.

"Then Rook and I will have to lower it manually."

The threat hung in the air, heavy and sweet like overripe fruit.

I closed my eyes.

Outside, the world was screaming. The internet was melting down. My quiet life as a biology student was dead and buried.

But inside the car, sandwiched between the monsters, the air was warm. The scent was right. And for the first time since I walked out of the dorm, the terrifying, hollow ache in my chest began to fill.

I wasn't a specimen anymore.

I was the keystone. And they had just cemented me into place.

Chapter Twenty-Two

THE VICIOUS PERIMETER

POV: Mercer

The noise on the other side of the double doors wasn't sound. It was heavy artillery.

It vibrated through the floorboards of the holding room, shaking the water in the plastic pitcher on the table. A thousand voices. A battalion of cameras. The world waiting to tear the meat from our bones.

Mina sat on the edge of the beige sofa. She wore the jersey we'd had made for her. Number 19 on the left, Number 24 on the right. It swallowed her. She looked like a child playing dress-up in a giant's armor. Her small hands gripped the hem, knuckles bleached white.

She smelled like terror.

The scent was sharp, acidic, cutting through her natural aroma of milk and vanilla. It hit the back of my throat like a swallowed razor.

"Stop shaking," I ordered. The words came out lower than intended, a rumble in my chest.

Mina flinched. Her big, wet eyes snapped to mine. "I'm trying."

"Don't try. Do."

Rook paced the length of the small room. Three strides up, turn, three strides back. He was a caged tiger, his tie ripped off and discarded on the floor, his top button undone to expose the thick column of his throat. He stopped in front of her. He loomed, blocking out the harsh fluorescent light.

"You smell scared," Rook growled. "I hate it."

"I'm ruining your career," she whispered. "They're going to take your 'A'. They're going to strip Mercer's 'C'. All because I let you—"

Rook dropped to his knees. The impact cracked against the linoleum. He grabbed her knees, ignoring the fabric, his thumbs digging into the soft flesh of her thighs.

"Shut up," Rook said. "Open your mouth."

Mina froze. Her lips parted.

Rook didn't kiss her. He leaned forward and inhaled, his nose brushing her chin. He breathed her in like oxygen in a submarine. His shoulders dropped an inch. The tension in his jaw slackened.

"Better," he grunted against her skin. "Focus on us. The noise out there? It's just static. We're the signal."

The door opened. The team PR director, a woman with a perpetually nervous tic in her left eye, stuck her head in. She looked at Rook on his knees between the girl's legs. She looked at me, standing guard like a gargoyle. She swallowed hard.

"It's time, Captain. Enforcer."

I moved.

I walked to the sofa and extended a hand. Mina stared at it. My palm was scarred, calloused from years of gripping a composite stick, wide enough to crush a skull.

She placed her hand in mine. It was impossibly small. Warm. Soft. It was the only thing in the world that didn't feel like a weapon.

I pulled her up. I didn't let go.

"Walk," I commanded.

We flanked her. Rook on her left, a wall of chaotic heat. Me on her right, a wall of cold iron. We marched her toward the noise.

"Remember the formation," I murmured as the security guard reached for the handle. "We are the perimeter. You are the asset. Nothing touches the asset."

The doors swung open.

Flashbulbs detonated. A blinding white supernova erupted in our faces. The roar of the press corps hit us like a physical wave, a wall of pressure trying to force us back.

Flash. Flash. Flash.

"Mercer! Is it true?"

"Rook! Look here! Left! Left!"

"Who is the girl? Is she a beard?"

"Are you still gay? Or was it all a lie?"

Mina stumbled. Her foot caught on the cable runner taped to the floor.

I didn't look down. I simply tightened my grip on her hand and hauled her upright. My arm brushed her shoulder, a heavy, silent reminder: *I have you.*

We reached the long table on the dais. Three chairs. Three microphones.

I sat in the center. Rook took the chair to my left. He didn't sit; he sprawled, legs spread wide, occupying as much space as physically possible. He glared at the sea of reporters, daring them to breathe wrong.

Mina hesitated. There was no chair for her.

I grabbed my thigh.

"Sit," I said.

The room went dead silent. The shutters stopped clicking for a microsecond.

Mina looked at the crowd, then at me. Her face burned crimson. But she sat. She perched on the edge of my thigh, her weight a negligible burden. She tried to make herself small, curling inward, but my hand landed on her hip, anchoring her to me.

"First question," I said into the mic. My voice was flat. Dead.

A man from the Tribune stood up. He looked smug. He smelled like cheap cologne and bad intentions.

"Captain Mercer," he started, his eyes flicking to Mina on my lap. "For three years, you and Rook have been the poster boys for the queer community in sports. You've claimed, repeatedly, that you have zero interest in women. That you are exclusively homosexual. Now..." He gestured vaguely at Mina. "This. Explain the contradiction."

I looked at the man. I imagined checking him into the boards at full speed. I imagined the sound his ribs would make.

"No contradiction," I said.

"Excuse me?" The reporter blinked. "She is clearly a woman."

I looked down at Mina. I looked at the curve of her jaw, the soft slope of her neck, the terrifying fragility of her wrist. I looked at the way her breasts pressed against the fabric of the jersey—*my* jersey.

I felt nothing for the women in the front row of the press pool. They were furniture. Background radiation.

But her? My blood ran hot, thick and sludgy with a dark, primal need.

"She isn't a woman," I said into the silence. "She is Mina."

Rook leaned into his mic. "We don't like girls," he rumbled, his voice scraping the bottom of the register. "We hate perfume. We hate the high-pitched noises. We hate the softness."

He reached over. His large hand covered Mina's other knee.

"But her?" Rook's lip curled, revealing teeth. "She's not a category. She's the exception that proves the rule."

"So, it's a polyamorous triad?" a woman from ESPN asked. "A throuple?"

"It is a dictatorship," I corrected. "We dictate where she goes. We dictate who touches her. And right now, the only people cleared for contact are sitting at this table."

"Is she a stress response?" someone shouted from the back. "A slump buster?"

Mina flinched. The insult landed. I felt her stiffen against my leg. A tear leaked out, hot and wet, landing on my hand where it gripped her hip.

That single drop of saltwater was the catalyst. The control snapped.

I stood up.

Mina gasped as I lifted her with me, tucking her against my side like a football. The microphone screeched feedback.

"Enough," I barked.

The room froze.

I looked into the cameras. I narrowed my eyes, broadcasting the threat directly into living rooms across the continent.

"You want a headline? Here it is." I pulled Mina closer, until her face was pressed into the expensive wool of my suit jacket. "We are selfish men. We take what we want. We wanted the Cup, so we took it. We wanted each other, so we took that too. Now?"

I looked down at the top of her blonde head.

"We want her. We don't care about the optics. We don't care about the definitions. She is the soft place where we land. She is the quiet in the noise. And if anyone prints a word that makes her cry again?"

I pointed at the Tribune reporter.

"I will find you. And I won't be wearing skates."

I didn't wait for questions.

"Move," I ordered Rook.

Rook didn't need telling. He was already up, shoving a cameraman aside with a sweep of his arm. We carved a path out of the room, leaving the chaos behind.

We didn't stop at the green room. We didn't stop at the car.

I dragged her into the nearest janitor's closet and kicked the door shut. The lock engaged with a deafening *click*.

Darkness.

The smell of bleach and old mops. And us.

Mina was sobbing. Quiet, hiccupping sounds that tore through my chest like shrapnel.

"I'm sorry," she wept. "I'm sorry, I'm sorry."

Rook grabbed her. He lifted her off the ground and slammed her back against the door. Not to hurt. To ground. To give her a solid surface in a spinning world.

Rook buried his face in her neck. He licked the salt from her skin, a desperate, hungry lapping.

"Stop apologizing," Rook growled against her throat. "You didn't do anything. You exist. That's enough."

"I made you say it," she cried, her hands tangling in Rook's hair. "I made you destroy everything."

"We destroyed nothing," I said.

I moved in. The space was too small for three people, but we made it work. We always made it work. I crowded her from the front, pressing her between the hard wall of the door and the harder wall of my body.

I reached for her face. My thumbs swept under her eyes, catching the tears. I brought them to my mouth. I tasted her sadness. Salty. Sweet. Mine.

"You think we care about them?" I asked, my voice dropping to a harsh whisper. "The fans? The league? They are noise, Mina. You are the only thing that is real."

"Show her," Rook demanded. He bit the soft spot where her neck met her shoulder. "Mercer. Fix her."

I didn't argue.

I gripped the hem of the jersey—my number, Rook's number—and shoved it up.

Mina gasped as the cool air hit her skin, followed instantly by the searing heat of my hands. I spanned her waist. My fingers nearly touched. She was so small. So breakable.

"Look at you," I murmured, staring at her exposed stomach in the dim light. "Soft. Pale. Useless for hockey. Useless for fighting."

I leaned down. I pressed a kiss to her naval.

"Perfect for us."

I dropped to my knees on the dirty concrete floor.

Rook stayed standing, pinning her arms above her head, locking her against the wood. He stared down at me, his eyes black holes of possession.

"Eat," Rook ordered.

I pushed her leggings down. The sound of fabric tearing filled the closet—I didn't have the patience for elastic.

She wasn't wearing panties. Good girl.

The scent hit me full force. Arousal. Fear. The specific, biological signature that rewired my brain every time I inhaled it. I groaned, a vibration that started in my soles and ended in my mouth.

I pressed my face into her softness.

Mina cried out, her head thumping back against the door. "Mercer, please. Not here."

"Here," I said against her wet heat. "Everywhere. Until you understand."

I licked her.

Not a gentle stroke. A claim. Broad and wet and heavy. I tasted the shock on her skin. I tasted the way her body betrayed her mind, swelling for me, weeping for me.

"Tell her," I commanded Rook, my voice muffled by her thighs.

Rook leaned down. He bit her lip, swallowing her cry.

"He's worshiping you, mouse," Rook rasped. "He's on his knees in the dirt. The Captain. The King. Kneeling for you."

I used my tongue. I found the bundle of nerves that made her forget her name. I worked it with the same relentless, punishing focus I applied to game tape. I analyzed the data—her hips bucking, her breath hitching, the tightening of her muscles—and I adjusted the pressure.

We weren't gay men in that moment. We weren't straight men. We were starving animals, and she was the only sustenance on the planet.

Mina shattered.

She screamed into Rook's mouth. Her legs clamped around my head, crushing my ears, trying to drown me in her release. I drank it. I swallowed every spasm, every drop, greedily cleaning the plate.

When she went limp, sliding down the door, I caught her.

I stood up, wiping my mouth with the back of my hand. I tasted like her. I would never wash my face again.

Mina hung between us, supported only by Rook's grip on her wrists and my arm around her waist. She looked wrecked. Ruined.

Beautiful.

"Do you understand now?" I asked, breathing hard.

She opened her eyes. They were glassy, unfocused, but the fear was gone. Burned away by the friction.

"Yes," she whispered violently.

"Say it."

"I'm the perimeter," she breathed.

"No," Rook corrected, smoothing her hair with a terrifying tenderness. "We are the perimeter. You are the heart."

I kissed her forehead. Then I kissed Rook's mouth, tasting her on his lips.

"We leave," I said. "We go home. We lock the door."

"And then?" Mina asked, her voice trembling with a different kind of anticipation.

I buttoned my jacket. I adjusted my cuffs. I looked at the two of them—my violence and my peace.

"Then we finish what we started on the table."

Chapter Twenty-Three

Muscle Memory

POV: Mina

The glass of the VIP box vibrated against my forehead.

Below, the ice was a blinding white sheet, scarred by steel and violence. The noise was absolute—a physical weight that pressed against my eardrums, composed of twenty thousand screaming fans, the grinding of skates, and the hollow *thwack* of composite sticks hitting a frozen rubber puck.

I didn't flinch. Two days ago, this chaos would have sent me retreating to the furthest corner of the library. Now, my pulse synced with the violence.

Down there, they were monsters.

Rook was a blur of black and gold, a heat-seeking missile made of muscle and bad intentions. He slammed an opposing winger into the boards directly below me. The impact shook the glass. The sound was a wet, heavy crunch that should have been sickening.

My thighs clenched.

A distinct, heavy throb started low in my belly, radiating outward until my knees felt weak. Warmth flooded the gusset of my panties, soaking the cotton. It was a conditioned response. Pavlov's dog, but instead of a bell, my trigger was the sight of Rook nearly decapitating a man who dared to touch the puck.

I pressed my hand against the cold glass.

I wore the jersey.

It was ridiculous. Obscene, really. Mercer had commissioned it overnight. The left half was number 19—Mercer. The right half was number 24—Rook. The seam down the middle was thick and stiff, a scar connecting two distinct halves of a single, lethal organism. It engulfed me, the hem hitting my mid-thigh, the sleeves rolled up four times to free my hands.

Wearing it felt like a claim. It felt like walking around with a collar that had their names engraved in brass.

"Kill him, Rook," I whispered, my breath fogging the glass.

On the ice, Rook disentangled himself from the heap of limbs. He didn't look at the referee. He didn't look at the scoreboard.

He looked up.

Through the distortion of the safety netting and the glare of the floodlights, he found me. He couldn't possibly see me clearly—I was a speck in the luxury box—but he knew where I was. He raised a gloved hand and tapped his chest, right over his heart. Then he pointed at the ice. *Stay.*

Mercer skated past him. The Captain. The ice king.

Mercer didn't look up. He didn't need to. He controlled the grid. He knew my coordinates the same way he knew the velocity of the puck. He circled the center line, barking orders, his posture rigid and commanding.

The crowd roared as the puck dropped.

I watched Mercer glide. He was mathematical perfection. Every stride was calculated to maximize force and minimize waste. He stole the puck with a surgical poke-check, pivot-turned, and accelerated.

My breath hitched. The air in the climate-controlled box felt suddenly thin.

Watching Mercer play was different from watching Rook. Rook was the blunt force trauma that broke me open; Mercer was the scalpel that rearranged my insides.

He crossed the blue line. Two defenders collapsed on him.

Rook hit them.

It wasn't a lawful check. It was a collision of freight trains. Rook cleared the path, his body acting as a battering ram, absorbing the impact so Mercer didn't have to break stride.

Mercer snapped his wrists. The puck vanished. The red light behind the goal exploded.

The arena dissolved into madness. The horn blared, a deep, resonant foghorn that vibrated in my teeth.

I didn't cheer. I couldn't. I was too busy trying to keep my legs from buckling. The sight of them working in tandem—Rook inevitably clearing the way, Mercer inevitably taking the shot—hot-wired my nervous system. It was exactly what they did to me in the dark. One to stretch, one to fill. One to hold me down, one to tear me apart.

My reflection in the glass looked wild. Pupils blown wide, lips swollen, chest heaving beneath the divided jersey. I looked wrecked. I looked like I belonged to them.

The period buzzer sounded.

I turned from the glass. I didn't wait for the handler. I knew the route.

I slipped out of the box, ignoring the stares of the wealthy donors in the corridor. They looked at the jersey. They looked at the girl who had been on the news, the "exception." Their gazes were curious, judgmental, hungry.

I didn't care. The only hunger that mattered was waiting for me at the ice level.

I took the service elevator down. The air grew colder with every floor, smelling sharper—ammonia, rubber, unwashed gear.

The tunnel was a concrete throat leading to the locker rooms. It was crowded with staff, equipment managers, and security, but the moment I stepped off the elevator, the atmosphere shifted.

The security guard, a massive man named Tiny who usually stopped everyone without a badge, spotted me. He stepped aside immediately.

"Ms. Mina," he grunted, opening the rope barrier.

"Thank you," I murmured, clutching the hem of my jersey.

I walked to the edge of the rubber mats. The team was coming off the ice.

The noise of skates on rubber was a rhythmic *clack-clack-clack*. The players were huge, hulking shapes in their bulky gear, smelling of sweat and aggression.

Rook came first.

He didn't walk; he stomped. He had his helmet in his hand, his hair plastered to his skull with sweat. Blood trickled from a cut on his eyebrow, mixing with the moisture on his face. He looked terrifying. He looked feral.

He saw me.

The scowl vanished, replaced by a dark, covetous heat that scorched me from ten feet away.

"Mouse," he barked.

He dropped his helmet. It clattered on the concrete. He didn't care.

Rook crossed the distance in two strides. He didn't care about the cameras. He didn't care about the sweat soaking his jersey or the blood on his face. He grabbed me.

His gloves were still on—stiff, stinking leather. He wrapped his arms around my waist and lifted me off the ground, burying his face in my neck.

"You watched," he rasped against my skin. He was hot—a furnace stoked to critical levels. The stench of him was overwhelming. Sharp, masculine, dirty.

I inhaled it greedily. "I watched."

"Did you see me hit him?" Rook demanded, pulling back to look at me. His eyes were wild, the pupils encroaching on the iris. "I put him in the wall for you. He looked at the box during warmups. I saw him."

"You hurt him because he looked at me?"

"I hurt him because he breathed in your direction," Rook corrected. He rubbed his cheek against mine, smearing sweat and blood onto my skin. He was marking me. Claiming the territory.

"Put her down, Rook."

The voice was cool, authoritative, and cut through the chaos like a blade.

Mercer stood behind him.

He hadn't removed his helmet yet. The cage obscured his face, turning him into a faceless machine of war. He loomed over us, his chest heaving slightly beneath the captain's "C".

Rook growled, a low vibration in his chest that I felt against my breasts, but he lowered me until my sneakers touched the rubber mat. He didn't let go of my waist.

Mercer reached up and unsnapped his chin strap. He pulled the helmet off, shaking out his damp hair. His blue eyes locked onto me. They were terrifyingly clear.

"Report," Mercer ordered softly.

"Heart rate one-twenty," I whispered, my hands finding the front of his chest protector. "Dampness... severe."

Mercer's nostrils flared. He leaned down, invading my space, crowding me against Rook's solid bulk.

"You liked the goal," Mercer stated. It wasn't a question.

"I liked the control," I confessed, my voice trembling. "I liked how you made everyone else look still."

Mercer's hand, still in the heavy glove, came up to cup my jaw. The leather was rough, cold from the ice, but his touch was reverent.

"Good girl," he murmured. "We play better when you watch. The variables align."

"You're bleeding," I noticed, reaching for Rook's eyebrow.

"Don't care," Rook grunted, turning his head to kiss my palm. His lips were chapped, hot. "Kiss it better."

I stood on my toes. Rook dipped his head. I pressed my lips to the cut, tasting the iron and the salt. It was gross. It was perfect.

A wolf-whistle echoed down the tunnel.

"Get a room, Cap!" one of the rookies shouted, laughing.

The air in the tunnel froze.

The tenderness evaporated from Mercer's face instantly. His expression hardened into granite. Rook stiffened against my back, his muscles coiling like springs under the heavy shoulder pads.

They turned in unison.

It was a synchronized movement of pure predator aggression. They didn't step away from me; they stepped *in*.

Rook moved to my left, angling his massive shoulder to block me from the team's view. Mercer moved to my right, creating a wall of composite armor and hostility. I was instantly eclipsed, hidden in the shadows of their bodies.

The laughter died. The rookie—a kid named Johnson—stopped walking. He paled.

Mercer didn't shout. He didn't need to. He simply stared, his eyes cold and dead.

"She is not for your entertainment," Mercer said. His voice was quiet, terrifyingly level. "She is not part of the locker room banter. Do not look at her. Do not speak to her."

Rook didn't speak. He just stared at Johnson, his hands flexing into fists, the leather gloves creaking under the strain. The violence rolled off him in waves, a physical heat that promised pain.

"I... sorry, Cap," Johnson stammered, looking at the floor. "Didn't mean anything."

"Walk," Mercer commanded.

The team filed past. They hugged the opposite wall, giving us a wide berth. Eyes stayed on the floor. No one dared to look at the small blonde woman sandwiched between the two giants.

When the last player had disappeared into the locker room, the tension didn't leave Mercer's shoulders.

He turned back to me. He looked at the jersey—his number, Rook's number. He looked at the blood on my cheek from Rook's face.

"Ours," Mercer whispered.

He reached out and hooked his finger into the collar of the jersey, pulling me forward until my chest bumped against the hard plastic of his chest protector.

"You wait in the car," Mercer ordered. "security will escort you."

"Why?" I asked, breathless.

"Because if you come into that locker room right now," Rook growled, leaning down so his lips brushed my ear, "we won't make it to the showers. We'll take you on the bench, right in front of them."

My core clenched. A fresh wave of heat slicked my thighs.

"Go," Mercer said, his eyes darkening as he smelled my reaction. "Before I stop caring about the felony charges for public indecency."

He kissed me—hard, fast, a seal of ownership that tasted of wintergreen and adrenaline—and then physically turned me toward the exit.

I walked away. My legs were shaking.

I didn't look back. I didn't need to. I could feel their gaze on my spine, heavy and tangible, tracking me until I was safely out of sight. I was the keystone, and the walls were finally holding.

Chapter Twenty-Four

Kneeling to Claim

POV: Mercer

The iron gates groaned, a heavy, industrial sound that signaled the end of the public world and the beginning of ours.

I watched the metal swing inward through the windshield of the Rover. Beside me, Rook tapped a restless rhythm on his thigh, his knuckles white, the energy rolling off him in waves of heat that the climate control couldn't mitigate.

"She's quiet," Rook rumbled, his voice low enough not to wake the woman in the backseat. "Too quiet."

I glanced in the rearview mirror. Mina was asleep. Her head rested against the cool leather, her blonde hair spilling over the seatbelt strap. She looked exhausted. The press tour, the games, the nights spent pinned between our bodies—it took a toll. She was resilient, but she was biological matter. She required rest.

"She is recharging," I said, guiding the car up the winding driveway. "Let her sleep until we stop."

The house rose out of the trees like a fortress. Modern. Sharp angles. Concrete and glass. It wasn't warm. It wasn't cozy. It was a structure designed to withstand sieges, nestled high enough in the hills that no telephoto lens could find an angle.

I parked in the circular drive. The gravel crunched under the tires, the sound sharp and final.

"Wake her," I ordered.

Rook didn't shake her. He reached back, unbuckled her belt, and simply lifted her out of the seat as if she weighed less than his equipment bag. Mina stirred, blinking against the afternoon sun, her hands instinctively clutching Rook's biceps.

"Are we here?" she mumbled, rubbing her eyes.

"We're home," Rook corrected.

I killed the engine. The silence that followed was absolute. No screaming fans. No reporters shouting questions about our sexuality or our sleeping arrangements. Just wind in the pines and the distant hum of the city we ruled.

I stepped out, adjusting my cuffs. The keys to the front door were heavy in my pocket. Brass. permanent.

Mina slid down from Rook's hold until her feet touched the gravel. She looked at the house, her eyes widening. Then she looked at me.

She didn't look at my face. Her gaze dropped.

She stared at my forearms, exposed where I'd rolled up the sleeves of my dress shirt. I saw her pupils dilate as she tracked the thick cables of veins running from my wrist to my elbow. Her eyes moved up, tracing the width of my shoulders, the way the cotton strained across my chest, the heavy line of my throat. It wasn't a sweet look. It was a consumption. She looked at me like I was a piece of prime steak and she hadn't eaten in a week. She wanted the violence promised by the muscle; she craved the weight of the bone structure.

My cock twitched. A hard, immediate response to being objectified by the one thing on earth small enough to break me.

"Like what you see?" I asked, my voice dropping an octave.

Mina didn't blush. She licked her lips. "I like that you're wide enough to block out the sun."

Rook laughed, a harsh bark of sound. He wrapped an arm around her waist, pulling her back against his chest. "Careful, mouse. You keep looking at him like that, we won't make it through the front door."

"Inside," I commanded, forcing my body to cool down. "We have business."

I unlocked the double doors. The mechanism turned with a satisfying *thunk*.

The foyer was cavernous. White marble floors, high ceilings, walls of glass looking out over the valley. It was empty. We hadn't moved furniture in yet. It smelled of new paint and money.

Mina stepped in. Her sneakers squeaked on the marble. She looked tiny in the vast space, a speck of color in a monochrome world.

"It's... big," she whispered.

"Four thousand square feet," I recited. "Perimeter security sensors. reinforced glass. Soundproofing in the master wing."

"Soundproofing?" She raised an eyebrow.

"Necessary," Rook grunted, closing the door behind us. "You get loud."

Mina walked to the center of the room. She spun slowly, taking it in. "Whose house is this? Are we renting it for a shoot?"

I walked to her. I stopped when the toes of my dress shoes touched the rubber of her sneakers.

"Not a rental," I said.

I reached into my pocket and pulled out the deed. I'd had the lawyers expedite it this morning. The paper was folded, thick and creamy.

I held it out.

Mina took it. Her fingers trembled slightly as she unfolded the document. She scanned the legal jargon, her brow furrowing. Then she stopped.

"Tenants in common," she read softly. "Mercer... Rook... and Mina?"

She looked up. Her face was pale. "My name is on the house."

"You need a habitat," I stated. logic was my shield. If I focused on the logistics, I wouldn't have to admit that my heart was hammering against my ribs like a trapped bird. "The dorm is insecure. The apartment was temporary. This is permanent."

"You bought me a house?"

"We bought *us* a house," Rook corrected. He came up behind her, resting his chin on top of her head. "Mercer did the math. Three bedrooms. One for sleeping. One for a gym."

"And the third?" she asked.

"East wing," I said, pointing down the hall. "Go look."

She hesitated, then walked down the corridor. Rook and I followed, silent shadows.

She pushed open the door at the end of the hall.

It wasn't a bedroom.

I had stripped it. The carpets were gone, replaced by chemical-resistant flooring. Along the far wall, a stainless steel workbench ran the length of the room. A high-end microscope sat under a dust cover. Beakers. Centrifuges. A ventilation hood.

It was a lab. A private, state-of-the-art biology lab.

Mina froze. She put a hand to her mouth. A small, choked sound escaped her throat.

"You said you needed space to think," I said, standing in the doorway. "You said we were suffocating you. That you couldn't work."

She walked to the microscope. She touched the cold metal as if it were a religious artifact.

"This is... this is insane," she whispered. "This equipment costs more than my tuition."

"Investments require maintenance," I said. "We are protecting our asset."

She turned around. Her eyes were wet.

"Stop it," she said fiercely. "Stop talking like I'm a stock portfolio. Stop talking like this is just logic."

"It is logic," I insisted, though my throat felt tight. "Variables explicitly state—"

"Mercer."

She crossed the room. She grabbed the lapels of my shirt and yanked. I didn't budge, but I leaned down, granting her the access she demanded.

"Tell me the truth," she demanded. "Why are we here? Why is my name on the deed?"

I looked at Rook.

He stood by the window, his arms crossed over his massive chest. He nodded. *Do it.*

I looked back at Mina. The softness. The steel. The only woman who didn't run when the monsters came out to play.

"Because the geometry fails without you," I rasped.

I stepped back.

I adjusted my trousers. Then, with deliberate slowness, I lowered myself.

One knee hit the floor. Then the other.

Mercer, the Captain, the man who never bowed to anyone, knelt on the hard floor of a sterile lab.

Rook moved. He didn't speak. He walked over and dropped down beside me. He didn't kneel gracefully; he sprawled, his heavy thighs spreading, sinking onto his knees with a thud that shook the floor.

We looked up at her.

Two giants. Two wealthy, violent, arrogant men. Kneeling at the feet of a biology student in a thrift-store hoodie.

Mina stared down at us. Her breath hitched.

"Mercer?" she squeaked.

"We don't do rings," I said. My voice was rough, scraping over the truth. "Rings are for people who need symbols. We deal in absolutes. Brick. Mortar. Blood."

I reached out and took her left hand. Rook took her right.

"We are broken things, Mina," I confessed. It was the hardest thing I had ever said. "Rook is chaos. I am rigidity. Without a center, we grind each other to dust. You are the fulcrum."

"You aren't a pet," Rook added, his voice thick with emotion. He pressed his face into her palm, kissing the lifeline. "You're the owner. We come with the house."

Mina looked from me to Rook. tears spilled over, tracking down her cheeks.

"You're asking me to keep you," she whispered.

"We are demanding it," I corrected softly. "We are surrendering our autonomy. We are handing you the leash. If you leave, we starve. If you stay..."

I squeezed her hand.

"If you stay, we will burn the world down to keep you warm."

The silence stretched. The air in the room grew heavy, charged with the scent of ozone and arousal.

Mina looked at the lab bench. She looked at the deed in her pocket. Then she looked down at us, her gaze turning molten.

She didn't pull her hands away. instead, she stepped closer. She stepped right into the space between us.

She released our hands and placed them on her head.

"Claim it," she whispered.

Rook groaned. He wrapped his arms around her waist, burying his face in her stomach.

I rose—not to my feet, but to my height on my knees. I grabbed her hips. I pulled her flush against my chest.

"Proposal accepted," I growled.

I kissed her. It wasn't gentle. It was a seal. A contract signed in saliva and breath. I tasted her salt. I tasted her acceptance.

Rook's hands roamed over her back, claiming the territory. "Bedroom," he muttered against her shirt. "Now. Christening."

"No furniture," she gasped, breaking the kiss.

"I'm the furniture," Rook said.

I stood up, lifting Mina with me. She wrapped her legs around my waist, lighter than air, heavier than the entire universe.

"Welcome home," I said against her throat.

I carried her out of the lab, Rook flanking me like a wolf guarding the pack. The front door was locked. The gate was closed.

The monsters were home. And we finally had our keeper.

Chapter Twenty-Five

The Only Vice

POV: Mina

The locker room smelled of cheap champagne, expensive sweat, and the metallic tang of victory.

Plastic sheeting covered the stalls, crinkling under the boots of thirty grown men who were currently screaming like children. Corks popped—gunshots in the enclosed space. Foam sprayed in arcs, soaking the carpet, the equipment, and the suits of the PR team huddled in the corner.

I stood near the medical table, my back pressed against the wall. I was soaked. My hair plastered to my skull, my vintage cardigan ruined, my skin sticky with the sugar of celebration.

I had never felt cleaner.

Rook was a monster in the center of the room. Shirtless, his torso a map of fresh bruises and old ink, he held the Stanley Cup above his head. Thirty-five pounds of silver looked like a toy in his grip. He roared, a sound that vibrated in the floorboards, and the team roared back.

Then, he stopped.

The silence that cut through the room was sudden and terrifying to anyone who didn't know him. To the rookies, it looked like rage. To me, it looked like a compass needle snapping North.

Rook lowered the Cup. He turned. His chest heaved, sweat tracking through the forest of hair on his pectorals. He didn't look at his teammates. He didn't look at the Coach.

He looked at me.

The crowd parted. They knew the hierarchy now. Even in the chaos of a championship win, the laws of physics in this room bent around the three of us.

Mercer appeared at Rook's side. The Captain. He still wore his skates, making him a tower of composite armor and authority. His face was bloodied—a high stick in the third period—but his blue eyes were glacial, calm, terrifyingly focused.

"Bring it here," Mercer ordered.

Rook marched. He carried the most coveted trophy in sports like it was a serving platter. He stopped in front of the medical table—the same table where they had first put their hands on me weeks ago.

Rook slammed the Cup down on the vinyl. The heavy *thud* shook the bottles of rubbing alcohol on the shelf.

Mercer stepped in. He gripped my waist. His gloves were gone, his hands rough and hot on my damp clothes. He didn't ask; he lifted.

I gasped as my feet left the floor. He deposited me on the table, right next to the silver chalice. My thigh pressed against the cold metal. The contrast shocked my system—the freezing burn of the trophy on one side, the searing heat of Mercer's body on the other.

"We don't drink alone," Mercer said. His voice was a low rasp, audible only to me and the man breathing down my neck.

Rook grabbed a magnum of champagne. He didn't bother with the cork; he used the edge of a skate blade lying on the bench to shear the top off. Glass shattered. Foam erupted.

He poured the liquid into the bowl of the Cup. It fizzed, rising to the rim, spilling over the engravings of names dead and gone.

"Drink," Rook commanded.

He gripped the back of my neck. His fingers were slippery with wine and violence. He tilted my head forward.

I leaned over the silver rim. The fumes of alcohol stung my nose. I drank. It was cold, sharp, and tasted like victory. I gulped it down, the bubbles burning my throat, until I had to pull back for air.

Liquor ran down my chin. It dripped onto my collarbone.

Rook made a noise—a guttural, starving sound. He dropped to his knees between my spread legs. He didn't care that the entire roster of the New York team was watching. He didn't care that ESPN was waiting outside.

He licked my throat.

His tongue was a rough, wet rasp. He chased the droplet of champagne down to the hollow of my throat, lapping it up with a possessive thoroughness that made my toes curl in my soaked sneakers.

"Sweet," Rook groaned against my skin. "Better than the win."

Mercer stood guard. He placed one hand on the Cup and the other on my knee, physically linking the three of us. A closed circuit.

I looked at him. The blood on his cheek was drying, cracking as his jaw worked.

"You did this," I whispered. "You won."

"We won," Mercer corrected. His thumb rubbed a slow, maddening circle on my inner thigh. "The data is conclusive, Mina. Before you? Chaos. Friction. Two alphas fighting for the same oxygen. With you?"

He looked down at Rook, who was currently pressing a kiss to the pulse point of my wrist.

"Structure," Mercer finished. "We needed a place to put the violence. You are the vault."

I looked at the Cup. I looked at the men.

The fear that had defined my life for twenty-one years—the fear of being too smart, too awkward, too soft for a hard world—evaporated. I wasn't just a biology student anymore. I wasn't a pet.

I was the clutch. I was the gear that turned the engine.

"Kiss me," I demanded.

Mercer didn't hesitate. He leaned down, capturing my mouth. He tasted of adrenaline and iron. It wasn't a gentle kiss. It was a claim, heavy and absolute. He devoured me, his tongue sweeping my mouth, taking everything I offered and demanding more.

Rook stood up. He didn't wait his turn. He moved behind me, his chest pressing against my back, sandwiching me between them. He buried his face in my hair, his arms wrapping around my waist, locking me in.

For a long moment, the locker room ceased to exist. There was only the heat of Rook's skin, the crushing weight of Mercer's mouth, and the cold, silent witness of the silver cup.

"Five minutes!" a voice barked from the doorway.

The spell fractured, but it didn't break.

Mercer pulled back an inch. His pupils were blown wide, black holes swallowing the blue. He didn't look at the PR director standing in the door. He kept his gaze pinned to mine.

"Five minutes," Mercer repeated, his voice dropping to a dangerous whisper. "Then we give them the photos. We give them the interviews."

"And then?" I asked, my lungs burning for air.

Rook bit the sensitive cord of my neck, marking me.

"Then we take the Cup home," Rook growled. "And we see if you fit inside it."

My core clenched. A heavy, wet heat flooded my system.

"We have a mansion," Mercer reminded him, wiping a smear of lipstick from his own mouth with his thumb. "We have a bed."

"Table is sturdier," Rook argued.

I laughed. The sound was bright, hysterical, and free.

I reached out, wrapping one arm around Mercer's neck and the other around Rook's thick bicep. I pulled them down, forcing the titans to bow.

"Take me home," I said. "I have a hypothesis I need to test."

Mercer's mouth curved. It wasn't a smile; it was a predator realizing the trap was actually a throne.

"Hypothesis accepted."

*

Epilogue

Twelve Months Later

The garden smelled of jasmine and money.

High walls of manicured hedging blocked out the world. The Los Angeles sun beat down on the white chairs arranged in precise rows on the lawn, but the heat couldn't touch the cool shade of the canopy where we stood.

I adjusted my dress.

It was white. Silk. Simple. Or, it would have been simple if not for the catastrophic alteration required at the waistline. The fabric stretched tight over the seven-month swell of my stomach.

My hand drifted to the bump. A kick answered—strong, impatient.

"He's awake," Rook murmured.

He stood to my left. He wasn't wearing a hockey jersey. He wore a tuxedo that cost more than my parents' house. The black fabric strained across his shoulders, the satin lapels catching the light. He looked uncomfortable, dangerous, and devastatingly handsome.

"She," Mercer corrected from my right. "Heart rate variability suggests female."

Mercer looked born in the suit. Rigid posture, hair swept back, checks sharp enough to cut glass. He held my right hand; Rook held my left.

We formed a line. A wall.

The officiant, a nervous man who clearly watched too much hockey, cleared his throat. He looked at the three of us. He looked at the guests—the team, the staff, the few family members who hadn't run for the hills when the *Vanity Fair* cover dropped.

"We are gathered here," the officiant began, his voice wavering, "to witness the union of Mercer and Rook..."

He paused. He looked at me.

"...and the commitment to the family they have built."

It wasn't a legal marriage for me. The laws hadn't caught up to our reality. Mercer and Rook were signing the papers. They were marrying each other. That was the public story. That was the headline. *Gay Hockey Icons Tie the Knot.*

But everyone in the front row knew the truth.

They knew why I was standing in the middle. They knew whose ring was on my finger—a thick band of platinum inset with two diamonds, one black, one clear.

Mercer turned to Rook.

"I take you," Mercer said. His voice didn't waver. "As my partner. My shield. My friction."

"I take you," Rook replied, his voice rough. "As my Captain. My anchor. My blood."

They didn't kiss. Not yet.

They turned inward. They turned to me.

The silence in the garden stretched tight. A bird sang in the distance, oblivious to the gravity of the moment.

Mercer reached out and placed his large hand on the top of my stomach. Rook placed his hand below it. Their fingers brushed against each other, encasing our child, encasing me.

"And you," Mercer whispered. The microphone didn't pick it up. It wasn't for the audience. "Mina. Our variable."

"We promise to keep the walls high," Rook swore, his dark eyes wet. "We promise to hunt for you. To kill for you. To bleed for you."

"We promise that you will never stand alone," Mercer added. "We are the tripod. Remove one leg, and we fall. We do not intend to fall."

Tears pricked my eyes. Hormones, maybe. Or maybe just the overwhelming, suffocating weight of being loved by two apex predators who had decided I was the only soft thing worth preserving.

"I promise to stay," I choked out. "I promise to be the place where you land."

Mercer leaned down. He kissed my forehead. Rook leaned down and kissed my cheek.

Then, finally, they looked at each other over the top of my head.

The connection between them crackled—electric, violent, essential. They were two halves of a weapon. I was the safety catch.

"You may kiss," the officiant whispered, sounding relieved to be done.

Mercer grabbed Rook's lapels. He pulled him in. They kissed—hard, deep, a clash of teeth that made the guests shift in their seats. It was aggressive. It was masculine. It was exactly who they were.

But they didn't break the circle. Their hands stayed on me. Their bodies boxed me in.

When they pulled apart, breathless, the crowd erupted. Applause. Cheers. The pop of champagne corks in the distance.

Rook looked down at me. He grinned, a boyish expression that took ten years off his scarred face.

"Cake time," he said. "The mouse needs sugar."

"The mouse needs to get off her feet," Mercer corrected. "Her ankles are swelling."

"I'm fine," I protested, though my lower back was screaming.

"You are carrying our legacy," Mercer said, his tone leaving no room for argument. "You will sit. We will serve."

They guided me down the aisle.

The photographer backpedaled, snapping furiously. I knew what the picture would look like. Mercer and Rook, tall and dark and imposing, walking in lockstep. And me, waddling slightly in the middle, glowing white and gold.

We reached the reception area. Mercer pulled out a chair—a throne, really, cushioned with velvet pillows he must have ordered specifically for today.

I sat. I placed my hands on my belly.

Rook knelt to adjust the hem of my dress. Mercer stood behind the chair, his hands resting on my shoulders, his thumbs digging into the tense muscle.

"Happy?" Mercer asked quietly, leaning down so his breath stirred the hair at my temple.

I looked out at the party. I looked at the ring on my hand. I looked at the two men who had terrified the world into accepting us.

"The data is conclusive," I said, leaning back into his touch.

Rook looked up from the floor. He rested his cheek against my knee.

"System functional," Rook murmured.

I smiled. The fear was a distant memory. The future was unwritten, complex, and probably messy. But in this moment, in the center of their gravity, everything was still.

"System optimal," I corrected.

And for the first time in my life, the math worked perfectly.

www.ingramcontent.com/pod-product-compliance
Lightning Source LLC
LaVergne TN
LVHW030920080826
845145LV00013B/2989

* 9 7 8 1 9 6 9 6 5 0 4 3 7 *